G R JORDAN

Culhwch Alpha

A Highlands and Islands Detective Thriller

First edition

ISBN: 978-1-914073-26-7

This book was professionally typeset on Reedsy.
Find out more at reedsy.com

Friendship and money: oil and water

MARIO PUZO

Contents

Foreword

This story is set on an oil rig, in the Cairngorms and on the Isle of Lewis. Although incorporating known cities, towns and villages, note that all events, persons, structures and specific places are fictional and not to be confused with actual buildings and structures which have been used as an inspirational canvas to tell a completely fictional story.

Acknowledgement

To Susan, Jean and Rosemary for your work in bringing this novel to completion, your time and effort is deeply appreciated.

Novels by G R Jordan

The Highlands and Islands Detective series (Crime)

1. Water's Edge
2. The Bothy
3. The Horror Weekend
4. The Small Ferry
5. Dead at Third Man
6. The Pirate Club
7. A Personal Agenda
8. A Just Punishment
9. The Numerous Deaths of Santa Claus
10. Our Gated Community
11. The Satchel
12. Culhwch Alpha
13. Fair Market Value

The Contessa Munroe Mysteries (Cozy Mystery)

1. Corpse Reviver
2. Frostbite
3. Cobra's Fang

The Patrick Smythe Series (Crime)

1. The Disappearance of Russell Hadleigh
2. The Graves of Calgary Bay
3. The Fairy Pools Gathering

Austerley & Kirkgordon Series (Fantasy)

1. Crescendo!
2. The Darkness at Dillingham
3. Dagon's Revenge
4. Ship of Doom

Supernatural and Elder Threat Assessment Agency (SETAA) Series (Fantasy)

1. Scarlett O'Meara: Beastmaster

Island Adventures Series (Cosy Fantasy Adventure)

1. Surface Tensions

Dark Wen Series (Horror Fantasy)

1. The Blasphemous Welcome
2. The Demon's Chalice

Chapter 1

David was tired. It had been a long couple of weeks, and frankly, the weather hadn't been great. Sure, every day might have given you a great view of the sea, but when you looked at the guard vessels bobbing up and down in the waves, sometimes you felt happy to be on the rig. You could feel the effects of the sea even this high up drilling for oil but compared to some of the guard vessels, they got it easy on the platform.

The platform in question was called Culhwch Alpha, the main platform for a relatively new field, far off the north coast of Scotland. A helicopter from Shetland had delivered him over two weeks previously to his role of platform manager. It was full on once he arrived and he was looking forward to his three weeks off, worry-free, back on dry land. You got into a mode, a way of it when life was simply work. And platform life also took its toll back on land.

It had been three years now since he had moved out, three years because he caught Margaret playing around for a solid year. She had been disappearing during his three weeks offshore. Maybe it was because the kids were growing up; maybe that gave her the opportunity, or maybe that was why she became bored. Whatever it was, it had caused irreparable damage to the marriage, and now he was struggling to find someone else. It was not that easy when you got to your late forties. You did not just pop out down the pub and pick someone up. Who was he kidding? He had not done that when he was in his twenties. Margaret had been a long-time friend before she became his wife. Now, she was his ex.

It's funny, David thought to himself, *the things that go through your head when you start doing your ablutions. Still, maybe it was like a little private fortress, space away from everyone.* He laughed to himself. Seeking refuge in a toilet, unbelievable. What had he come to? His salary commanded much more than that.

A shrill alarm hit the air, and David groaned. There was the call-to-muster. Everyone had to gather on the platform. Something had happened. Maybe it was a leak, maybe it was a small fire. Who knew? It was something, and he would find out soon enough, but he needed to move quickly. He cleaned up and dressed himself, and not pausing to wash his hands, made his way out to the main muster point of the platform.

David could see the men arriving already, gathering as boards were produced and people's names were ticked off by his deputies. So many platform personnel they had to count the numbers. Meanwhile, he approached Andrea, who would have been in the control room when the alarm went off.

'I'm not sure, David, before you ask. I'm not sure, but we think it's a small fire on the far side of the platform. I'm sending a small group out to look for it now.'

'You've got the names of those people?'

'Of course. Just going through the head count of everybody else now.'

David looked around him. Had everyone gathered? There

2

was no way with the number of personnel on the platform that he could simply look around and know everyone was there. He would have to wait until the counts were done. Recalling his own role, David made the call to land, advising the coastguard that he had gone to muster. It would probably be nothing. It wasn't like false alarms didn't happen, but the trouble with the platform was that if it wasn't nothing, it might be a real fire. You had to be careful. Things got out of hand quickly, and then you were out in the middle of nowhere with the sea all around you, praying the guard vessel could get to you.

Andrea came rushing up to David, shaking her head. 'We've got about five people missing,' she said.

'About five?'

'We're still counting the numbers. We've got at least five missing. Still waiting for a couple to come back with their headcounts.'

'Get them done sharpish. Any word from the team sent out?'

'Not yet,' said Andrea, 'expecting any minute.'

'Okay,' said David. 'Let's not panic here. Let's keep it nice and routine like it always is. Somebody set something off, it's what usually happens.' Andrea nodded, but David could see a slight worry in her eye. There was always that worry in the background, that voice that said, *What if this is the real one? What if this is the one that does go wrong?* Of all the many instances they trained for on the platform, so many rarely came to pass. How many rigs had been destroyed, had blown up, or caught fire? Sure, everyone remembered Piper Alpha, but in truth, the offshore industry was incredibly safe, heavily regulated. Most importantly, it was very well paid.

There was nothing for David to do but wait until he got the final head counts and could find out what he was dealing with from the team who were out seeking the issue. His mind should not have, but it drifted. He was thinking about the holiday he was going to go on in two months' time. It was a simple one, just somewhere out in the sun on the beaches of Spain, but maybe there, he could find someone if even for just a short time. That was the thing about the divorce. Did he miss Margaret? Of course, he did, but he missed her in lots of ways, and he knew over the last year, he had been much more tense than he had ever been. Even back in the time when he knew she was playing around, it had taken him six months to confront her, six months of him coming out here knowing that she was with someone else. . . and in truth, they both knew.

Andrea came rushing up again. 'It's okay, David. It's okay. It was a small fire. They've put it out. They're checking around it now, but it seems all okay. Nothing much to worry about.'

'We'll have to check how it started,' he said. 'Any initial ideas?' Andrea shook her head.

'I've only just received the team's report. They're checking the area, making sure it's safe, so we'll keep everybody in muster, David. Let them go in a minute, but we're also short, short on the muster.'

'How short? I mean, where are they?'

· 'We're one short. There's a number of them arrived late, but I'm not sure why. We need to look into that, but we're definitely one person short.'

'Are you sure we're safe in terms of the platform. The fire's definitely out?'

'Yes,' said Andrea. 'The team said it's okay. They're just checking for other ignition sources just to make sure nothing's left to chance.'

'Right. Assemble a team. You'll take them around and we'll look for this other guy. Who is it anyway?'

'Angus Macleod, part of the canteen staff. The chef said he saw him, called him to go. In fact, the chef believes he'd left the kitchen.'

'Okay. Grab a team together, Andrea. Go and find him. Give me a call when you know what's what.'

Bloody magic, thought David. *A little routine thing like this and some asshole goes and gets himself hidden away. He's probably fallen and broken his leg somewhere. Panicked, flipping kitchen staff. That's the thing. These guys didn't come out to a rig because they were proper off-shore workers. No. They were just chefs or people who couldn't find a job elsewhere or who'd decided to cook for a better living. Still, something has happened to him. If he did break a leg or twist an ankle, it's more flipping paperwork.'*

David made his way out amongst the muster groups and began talking to the staff assigned to each of the group. He explained what was going on and the fact that they should all be back to work in the next ten or fifteen minutes. After that, he made the phone call to land, explaining they would be standing down the muster very soon, that it looked like not a false alarm but a very minor incident. With that done, David picked up a bottle of water, took a long drink, and breathed in deeply. He was looking forward to Spain, time to sit and survey the beaches, time away from this, maybe time with a woman he would find over there. She would probably be a divorcee, too, forty-something. There would be no worries about long-term relationships or anything— both just needing a bit of fun. Yes, that was what he wanted.

While David was deep in happy thought, a bald man ran up to him, one he thought he recognized but was not convinced.

'A message from Andrea. You need to come and see. You need to come and see.'

'Why? What's up?' asked David.

'I don't want to say here,' said the bald-headed man.

'It's— what's your name again?'

'John, but Andrea, she says you need to come now.'

'Can I let down the muster though?' asked David. 'We'll send everybody back if you've found him.'

'No,' said the man. 'Don't. She said whatever you do, keep everyone together. Tell David just to come, just David.'

'Where? Go where?'

'To the kitchen,' said the man. 'Go to the kitchen. I'll tell the rest of them we're holding muster here and to prepare for a long one. You need to go to the kitchen, David.'

'Why?' asked David, but the man seemed unable to speak.

David shook his head. What was it with people? You just say what it is. It wasn't like he couldn't handle anything. Making his way along the gangways and then corridors to the canteen area, David was amazed about how quiet everything was. Usually, you could not walk anywhere in the platform without bumping into someone, but now everyone was mustered together. It was almost like coming onto the rig for the first time when they towed it out before it found its final place. Culhwch Alpha was a relatively new platform in a field far off the north coast of Scotland. It was named Culhwch after one of the ancient Britons, like so many of the other platform fields, and this was the first platform to be established.

There was a Bravo some distance away and a Charlie was planned, but there would be a number of factors governing whether Charlie went ahead. It was a crazy life out here, high above the sea with nothing around you except the odd safety vessel. Occasionally, you got commercial traffic going by, but he thought on this platform, it seemed to be less so. They seemed to be more remote, if you could be more remote in the sea. Maybe they were just further away from the more obvious shipping lanes.

David turned around the corner to the double doors that led into the canteen. As he pushed them open, he saw some of the team that had made their way with Andrea to search for the missing man, and the shock on their faces did not look good. One had tears in their eyes and was being comforted by a colleague. In some ways, it looked a little strange to David. He'd grown up with the man being the strong one of the household, expecting a woman to cry on his shoulder, but here he had a brown-haired colleague, maybe six foot, weeping tears into the shoulders of a smaller, female colleague. She looked up at David, shaking her head gently but saying nothing.

'Andrea, what the hell is going on?' asked David. 'What's the matter?'

'Through the kitchen, David. You need to come. Prepare yourself.'

'Prepare myself? What do you mean, prepare myself?' David pushed open the door into the kitchen and saw Andrea on the far side staring across at something behind the large ovens. They were blocking David's view, and clearly, Andrea was looking at something of a horror. Her face was in shock and her normally tanned skin had turned to white.

'He just was like this when we got here, just like this. I didn't do anything. I haven't touched anything. Well, that table over there— that's on its side because James stumbled, fell on it. Other than that, we haven't touched anything. I don't think

7

we should touch anything.'

'What do you mean?' said David. 'Why wouldn't we touch anything? What-' Something caught David's eye. At first, it was a blurred, dark shape in the corner of his left eye, one second there, the next not. David quickened his step to look around the corner of the ovens, and then he saw two legs. He followed them up to the torso of a man and a head lying to one side on his shoulder. Around the neck was a piece of electrical wire that ran up into the ceiling of the kitchen. Something was causing the man to swing ever so gently. Maybe it was the vibration of the platform. At this point in time, David could not think what would cause it, but instead, he stared in horror at the body drifting slowly backwards and forwards.

'Is he all right?' asked David.

'All right?' said Andrea. 'He's bloody dead. Look at him. He's bloody dead.'

'How do you know?' said David. 'Has anybody touched him? Has anybody?'

David saw the angle of the neck. Surely no one alive would have a neck at that angle. At the very least it was broken.

'I tried for a pulse,' said Andrea, 'but I couldn't find anything on his wrist. I'm not touching the neck, but he's dead and somebody has killed him. You don't do that.'

'It could have been a suicide.'

'It's no suicide. It's no bloody suicide, David. Look at it. Look at the wire.'

David walked around to the back of the body. The electrical wire disappeared up into the ceiling but then re-emerged about two feet away where it ran in a straight line before being tied to a leg of a table. The table had all sorts of heavy food items on it, buckets of flour and sugar.

'It's anchored, David. They knew that wouldn't move. You can't move that table without taking that stuff off. Somebody knew what they were doing. They've put him up there.'

'Who? Why?' cried David. 'What the hell? Why would anyone want to kill this guy? Who is he even? I mean, I know there's people with issues in this place, but it's an oil platform. You just get on with it. You go home. You take your money. What the hell's this?'

'It's murder,' said Andrea. 'That's what it is. It's bloody murder. There's a killer amongst us. I'm telling you, David; there's a killer amongst us.'

Chapter 2

Hope felt the hand run up the side of her thigh, then across her hip before tracing a line up towards her back and then to her neck. The hand started to rub her skin. She gave out a little moan and felt the tension subside. Opening her eyes, she stared across at a clock she barely recognized. It was an electric alarm clock, its digits looking back at her, 14:30. *Half two in the afternoon*, thought Hope. *Just as well it's my day off.* She felt another hand this time tracing the other side of her and soon she felt the body of the man the hands belonged to. His arms snaked around her holding her tight causing her to smile.

It had been a month since he'd first taken her out. It had not been glamorous. She had said, 'Just the cinema. Just to go see a film.' In fact, she was glad they had not been anywhere glamorous. Hope had had enough of being wined and dined. With the way her last relationships had gone, she wanted something grounded in the normal, the everyday, the mundane. She wanted to see if he were right for her, not what he could afford.

'Do you fancy a walk?' said Hope. 'I need to stretch my legs. I need to just. . .'

'Just what?' said the man. 'I need to just walk and smile and just think how good this is. That doesn't sound like you.'

'I like walking,' said Hope. 'You know I like walking. We've gone out on a walk before.'

'Not the walk— the talk,' said the man. 'You don't say things like that.'

'No, I don't,' she said. 'But I do need to smile. I do. I just want to enjoy this.'

'I'm enjoying it right now,' said the man, and gave her a cheeky smack on the bottom. Hope grinned.

'Let's just get up and walk and enjoy the air. We've been in this bed all morning.'

'Do you want to shower?' asked the man.

'Of course, I do,' said Hope and reached back with her hand to tap him on the hip. 'Come on, let's have a shower.' With that, she stepped out of the bed not caring about her state of undress and made her way to the bathroom hearing him follow. As he reached the door, Hope heard the worst sound she could imagine. The doorbell rang.

'Don't get it' said Hope 'Just get in here.'

'I can look from the window,' said the man.

'John,' said Hope, 'Get in here.'

'Might be important. Could be for you. You know you sometimes get called away on stuff. I mean, don't you? You did warn me about that. You did say if you suddenly disappear, and I didn't get a call, you would probably have been called off on a case. Sometimes you can't call. Sometimes you can't react that quick to let me know.'

'If it's them, they'll phone,' said Hope. 'Besides, they don't even know I'm here. It's probably somebody dropping off a parcel for you or that.'

'I haven't ordered any parcel,' said John. 'I'll just check.'

'Is this not good enough for you?' said Hope turning around and standing in front of the man. 'I mean I don't want to boast but usually most men come running into the shower when I'm like this.'

'So would I, but you know it's an important job you do.'

'Would you get over that?' said Hope. 'Of course, I know; I do the bloody job.' Then she heard her phone vibrate. 'Bollocks,' she said out loud. 'Bollocks, bollocks, bollocks.' She watched John make his way over to the window carefully looking out so as not to show his nakedness to anyone outside.

'There's a man at the door.'

'What's he look like?' asked Hope.

'He's a fair bit older than you. Quite serious looking. Bit of a dark suit.'

'Why Seoras? Why now?' said Hope to the air. 'Why on earth?'

'Do you want me to go down and speak to him?'

'I'll get the intercom,' said Hope and walked across the flat pressing a button on the side. 'You have got to be kidding me, Seoras. How did you find me?'

'I'm sorry,' said the soft-spoken voice, 'but it's important Hope. We've got a dead man on an oil platform. We need to get moving as we're going to get helicoptered out. I couldn't wait. I hope I didn't interrupt anything.'

Hope looked across at John Allen, the man who for the last month had been making her extremely happy. This was the first night that they had become intimate. Here she was in the aftermath of it wanting to enjoy its glow and the job once again interrupts.

'You'll have to give me a minute,' said Hope. 'I need to get changed.' There was an awkward cough on the other end of the coms. 'I'd say come up, Seoras, but there's not a lot of room up here and we're not really in a state for coffee.' Again, there was another little cough.

'I'll be in the car but get a move on, Hope. We need to get to the airport sharpish. We're flying up to Shetland. From Shetland, we're heading out. Pack a bag.'

'Bag's in the boot as ever, boss.' With that, Hope took her finger off the comms button and looked across at John. She watched him stare at her before making his way across, putting his arms around her and giving her a hug. They kissed for a moment before he stepped away, telling her to get dressed.

'Go catch him then, said John, 'I'll see you when you're back. I'm your first call, though. I don't want to hear you're going off somewhere else. Popped off to get yourself a cheeseburger ahead of me.'

'Cheeseburger?' said Hope. 'What on earth?' She laughed. He was like that with his daft comments. 'Just keep the bed warm,' said Hope. 'I'll be back.'

'You'll be back for the walk you've just asked me for, first.'

Hope smiled. 'Always in the way— this ruddy job, always in the way.'

* * *

'I never pictured you as somebody who wanted a car-rental manager,' said Macleod. 'Nice steady job. Nice steady man by the sounds of it.'

'I didn't pick him because of his job,' said Hope. 'I picked him because he's interested in me. I picked him because, well, when we're doing the boring things, I still want to be there.'

Macleod nodded and looked around the small terminal as they waited for the aircraft. 'That sounds good. I spend nights in with Jane at times and we don't do anything. Not even any of that, before your mind gets there, and I'm happy. Sounds like you're going about this the right way.'

'Well, thanks for the relationship advice, Seoras. I'm deeply touched, and obviously, you're the first person I'd go to for it.'

Macleod looked at Hope as she grinned at him. 'There's no need to be sarcastic,' he said. 'I'm genuinely happy for you. I hope it works. I really do. You've taken enough bad punches on that side.'

'I've taken more than enough punches in this line of work. For once, could you not find me? You could have just gone. Why couldn't you take Kirsten with you? What was the problem with taking Kirsten, anyway?'

'Kirsten's brother's not very well. I couldn't be guaranteed to get her back off the rig quickly if something happened. I wanted Ross left in the office and you know why. Ross is good at organizing everything. I have a feeling there's a lot going to need to be organized with this. We've got a body on an oil rig. I've got Jona coming out with us and another of our team but just getting her stuff out there's a nightmare. We could be a couple of days at least sorting out the crime scene and doing the interviews. I don't want to wait until everybody comes back off their shift.'

'Well, when does their shift end?'

'Well, it depends, it's not like everybody just piles out, and everyone piles back in again,' said Macleod. 'Chefs work three weeks on, three weeks off for most of them depending on who they're employed by but with the helicopter runs, the timing start of your three-week shift is different to somebody else.'

'There's hundreds of people out on this platform and we've got a murderer amongst them,' said Hope. 'We're looking to try and spot the murderer amongst hundreds.'

'It's not so bad,' said Macleod. 'Normally the murder occurs in Scotland. You're starting off with over six million. At least out there, it's unlikely anybody from the mainland took a swim out to finish him off.'

Macleod was being very jovial, thought Hope. She wondered why. Maybe it was that he was happy for her. Maybe he had that giddy feeling that men sometimes got when they saw a close friend getting somewhere with a partner. It was unlike him. If he was going to be happy on this trip, it'd be better than working with a miserable Macleod over there.

Jona arrived with her assistant and the four officers flew up to Shetland on the small Saab 340 aircraft. Macleod had flown several times around the islands but Hope was always surprised by how nervous he got. These planes were old workhorses. She remembered someone telling her that they would rather fly in one of these that have done so many landings in the worst of weather than in something brand new that hadn't been tested. There was something in that. It was just that when you looked at them, you didn't always feel that safe.

They had a short wait in Shetland before stepping onto a helicopter that would take them out to the oil rig. They went through a briefing and had life jackets handed to them before stepping onto the helicopter. Most people who flew out to the rigs had to go through training so, if the helicopter ditched, they knew how to get out of it, but there was no time for that. Instead, the four officers were taken through a brief safety talk before being escorted out to the helicopter. As they flew over

15

the wide expanse of sea, Hope saw Jona touch Macleod's knee and tried to speak to him above the noise of the helicopter.

'What's the weather like for the next couple of days? How quick do we need to get away? Are their helicopters going to be flying?'

'I'm not sure it's going to be great for the next while,' said Macleod. 'The next twenty-four hours look very good but then the weather's looking like it will worsen. The quicker we do this, the better. Besides, I don't fancy spending too long out on a rig. I do have a life.'

So do I now, thought Hope. *I've finally got someone to come back to. I might not even go back to my own house.* She glanced up at Jona, the Asian woman she shared her house with. The young Japanese woman had not seen her the last two days. There was a knowing smile from Jona when they had met, and Hope had grinned back, and they knew everything had gone well.

Beside Jona was a man of maybe twenty-five who had recently transferred up to the scenes of crime in Inverness. His name was Alan Corrin. He had come highly recommended and had followed a curve like Jona had, progressing fast. Hope thought he was maybe in for one of his toughest challenges yet. Assuming they got accommodations, Hope reckoned, they would probably have to share. That was what she had heard about the rigs. The accommodation was good, but it wasn't exactly a hotel. They would probably have to double up. The obvious thing was for Jona and Hope to go together.

Hope was waiting to see how the boss would set up an incident room on an oil platform but he looked to have a good frame of mind and that was always the best way to start an investigation. As they approached the oil rig, the sun was beginning to set, and Hope saw the light glint off the side of it. The sea was a slick caramel colour as the helicopter touched down on the large H set to one side of the platform. The four officers were escorted off, the whirr of the rotor blades above them, and taken into a small room where a man stepped forward to shake Macleod's hand. 'I'm David McCallan, platform manager.'

'Detective Inspector Macleod. This is Detective Sergeant Hope McGrath. These are Forensic Officers Jona Nakamura and Alan Corrin. I'm going to need some accommodation, Mr McCallan, and I'm going to need to set up a small incident room. I realize you might not have a lot of space here, but you're going to have to make it.'

'I'll do whatever I can to help you, sir,' said David McCallan. 'I need to give you a brief about what we're doing here, and about emergency procedures. It's part of the job. I don't wish to hold you up, but the sooner I do it, the quicker you can get on to do whatever you need to do.'

'By all means,' said Macleod. 'If you show us our accommodation or throw our stuff in there, it needs to be locked accommodation. I take it that's the case.' The man nodded. 'Good. Then you can give us a brief and we'll get on.'

The man turned to a couple of his colleagues and pointed towards Jona, who had many bags with her. The platform workers picked up the bags and followed McCallan as he led the four officers through a small maze to their accommodation. Hope looked around and noted the stares as they walked past the various people going about their daily jobs.

'Seoras,' she whispered. 'Are you seeing that? Plenty of eyes on us.'

'Yes, I can see it. What do you expect? They know they've

17

got a killer amongst them.'

'I've never worked on a platform. I don't know what they're like.'

McCallan showed the four officers to their accommodation, and as Hope stepped into hers, dropping her bag inside, she saw the two bunks, some wardrobe space, and a small desk.

'Well, this looks cosy,' said Jona, as she pointed out, where the many bags brought by the platform workers should be stored.

'We'll need to get to somewhere to work,' said Hope. 'You're not going to be able to look at bodies in here, and I'm not sleeping beside a cadaver.'

'You always get squeamish around bodies,' said Jona. 'They're the safest people. You guys deal with the people that kill us. I deal with the people that just don't do anything. They simply lay there. I'll never understand you.'

Hope raised an eyebrow. 'I'm still not sleeping beside any dead body.'

Macleod stuck his head in. 'Next door please, soon as,' said Macleod. 'I want to give a small briefing before we head off for our induction.'

Two minutes later, Hope sat in the plastic chair in an identical room to the one she had just left. Macleod was standing with his back to his bunk and allowed the two women to sit down while Alan Corrin was standing against the opposite wall.

'Before we go any further,' said Macleod, 'I just want you to be aware. I've never been on an oil rig. I'm used to going into strange estates, high-class places, bars, strip joints, factories, wherever on the mainland, but I don't know how this place runs. I don't understand this community and it's going to be our first thing to find out what sort of community is here. Why would you kill someone out here? Who knows who? Who interacts with who? That's what we need to know, but let's not forget. Who knows who on the mainland as well? They're here for three weeks, but they're back there for three weeks. Are the lives interconnected? We need to find out, and I'm not sure how much cooperation we're going to get. You probably noted the stares as we came along. We're intruding on their patch, but I want to be clear, this is a murder investigation. It's just somewhere different. We are the law here. They might have the rules, they might have the safe ways of doing things, but we say what goes when it comes to the investigation.

'We say who we talk to, when we talk to them, and they have to sort out how they get around that. I don't care if I have to shut this rig down. We have a murder and until we find the guilty party, we run this as we run anything on land. Am I clear?'

'Well, you won't get any complaints from me,' said Jona. 'I don't mind working in tight spaces, but I'm going to need somewhere separate and we're going to need a proper lock-up. We haven't got anybody to protect the scene either.'

'No, we don't,' said Macleod. 'We don't even know what state the scene is in, so after he gives us this induction, you go straight there, Jona, and if you need to close it off, you close it off. Now, best of order when we go to this man's briefing. If he takes more than half an hour, I'm going to cut him short, but until then, business faces and anything reasonable he asks in terms of safety, we do. Anything that impedes the investigation, we kick back.'

There was a consensus and a general murmuring which seemed to satisfy Macleod. Jona departed with her assistant and Macleod stopped Hope before she left the room as well. 'We're on uncharted ground here, Hope, so any ideas, don't hesitate to say them. If you think I've gone off in the wrong direction, don't hesitate to tell me.'

'It's not like you, sir. You're usually pretty confident and sure of yourself, Seoras.'

'We all get knocked off when we're not on home turf,' said Macleod. 'Trust me, this does not feel like home turf.'

Chapter 3

'Well, that's thirty minutes of my life I'm not getting back,' said Hope. Macleod raised his eyebrows, not impressed with the comment from his senior partner.

'It's what we do and if something happened, I wouldn't know what to do, so let's not be saying comments like that to them. There's hard enough questions to ask here without starting people off on the wrong foot.'

'That's remarkably generous of you, Seoras. It's not like you to say something like that.'

'As I said before, the territory's unfamiliar, but there was a lot of closed expressions when we walked onto this rig. There may be more to come. Let's not put any there by our attitude.'

Macleod smiled politely as David McCallan escorted the four officers to the canteen. The busy hubbub of the rig was continuing and Macleod noticed many people walking here and there as he approached the canteen. Inside, he could hear noises.

'Do you have a double set up then?' asked Macleod. 'Two working kitchens? Two canteens?'

'No,' said Mr McCallan. 'It's only the one.'

Macleod's heart sank. 'By the sounds of it, sir, that canteen is in use.'

'Oh, yes. Look how many people I've got here. You have to feed them. It's been over eight hours since he died. I can't just have people starving. We've been out working on the rig. You just don't keep a platform like this down. You have to keep churning the oil out. Time's money, inspector.'

'That, sir, is a crime scene, one that you've just contaminated. I've brought a forensic officer along, someone to come in, look for fingerprints, hair, other fragments, anything that might indicate who the killer is, and you just let everybody right back in?'

'No,' said David McCallan, 'not just everybody back in. Come, I'll show you.' The man opened the double doors to the canteen and Macleod saw many tables with plastic chairs around them. There was a large group of men eating at these with the occasional woman dotted here and there. Something in Macleod's head had said that it would be entirely men out of the rig, but clearly, that wasn't the case. Maybe that was a different line to think about when it came to the murder.

'Doesn't seem to be much cordoning off here, sir,' said Macleod.

'Not in here. In the kitchen. I think you'll find we've done well with it.' David McCallan made his way to a door at the side of the canteen hatch pushing it open and entering the kitchen area. There were stainless steel tables everywhere as well as ovens and fryers and large fridges on the far side. 'This is where I came in, inspector. Just about here, I could see his feet swinging. When you went around that corner over there, you'll see where he was hanging from the ceiling.'

Macleod looked around. Dinner was in full swing with chefs

cooking and transporting goods about. A couple of them were giving a hard tut at the new arrivals.

'Chef, this is Inspector Macleod. He and his team are here to investigate what happened to Angus. I want you to give him every cooperation you can.' Macleod shook hands with the head chef. He didn't smile but instead nodded to a direction past the ovens.

'Over there, inspector. There you'll find where he was. Wasn't there when I left. Wasn't there when I came back either. Taken him down by then.'

'You've taken him down?' queried Macleod. 'I understood that somebody checked the pulse. You decided the man was dead in the hanging position. Who said you could take him down?'

David McCallan frowned at Macleod. 'You can't expect these people to come in here and cook with a body swinging about, can you?'

'This is a crime scene, sir. You shouldn't have done anything before we got here and anything you were going to do, you should have asked. I could understand if the body was brought down if you were trying to check if he was alive, but having decided he was dead, you've now tampered with the body. Makes the job much harder.' Macleod could see Jona walking on ahead around the corner of the ovens and the Asian woman shook her head.

'Inspector, I'm not sure what I'll get from this. I'll do what I can. Where is he?'

'Who?' asked David McCallan.

'She means Angus Macleod, the dead man, sir. Where is the dead man?'

'Oh, he's out in the chill. We've wrapped him up.'

'You put him in the chill?' said Jona. 'No, no, no. You don't do that.'

'Do you not have procedures to follow, sir?' asked Macleod. 'I'd have thought this would be written down.'

'What? Procedures in what to do if there's a murder? I mean, if somebody drops dead, we usually call. We get them evacuated off. There's no rush, but we don't have anywhere talking about a murder.'

Macleod turned to Hope. 'McGrath, get this place fenced off. Give Jona a hand. Get it as tight as you can, so our colleagues can get to work. Find the body. Put it where Jona wants it. Mr McCallan, I want a room for my forensic people, somewhere they can put stuff into, somewhere they can lock up.'

'We gave you your accommodations.'

'You want me to put a body in with people sleeping?'

'Of course not,' said McCallan. 'We're keeping him in the cold store.'

'No, you won't. You'll find me a room and we'll be putting the body in that room, and there, Ms Nakamura can work on him and decide what was going on here. You'll also provide me with a room where I can interview people.'

'Inspector, this is an oil rig. We just don't have random bits of accommodation lying around.'

'This, sir, is a murder scene. You were the one who said his neck was broken. It's a murder scene. This is a murder inquiry and while I might only have four officers here, I still require space aside to interview suspects. You may very well have a killer walking amongst you.'

McCallan shrunk back. 'I'll see what I can do for you, Inspector, but I can't promise much in the way of space.'

'You will give me space,' said Macleod. 'Shift people, whatever. Unless it's operationally necessary, you will shift rooms for me. Do you understand me?'

The man nodded and hurried off.

'Is it all right if I can get past?' said the chef. 'Just behind where he was, you got the table with all the salt on that one. It's quite important, those ingredients.'

'Sir,' said Hope, 'that wire is attached to that table. That's part of the evidence.'

'Haven't you got any more salt and sugar and things you can use for the meantime?' asked Macleod.

'It's all in the store, large packets of it. We don't use that though. You can get cross-contamination. That's bits of packet that you ripped open and then they end up in the food.'

'Well, you just have to take a risk,' said Macleod. 'Go and get it. Put it somewhere else in here. If that's too much of a problem, it's fine. I'll shut the kitchen. In fact, I'll take everybody off this rig, if I have to.'

The staff in the kitchen looked at Macleod as if he was off his head. He stared at each and every one of them and tried to lay down a marker. Once he'd done so, he followed Hope over to see where the crime had taken place.

'Well, I like the way you're smoothly moving in, making sure we don't upset anybody unnecessarily.'

Macleod glared at Hope and he said, 'I can't believe this.'

'There's the wire, sir. It's electrical wire. Looks like it's been pulled out of the socket up above. It's come down and it's been fed back up over something and attached to that table. Looks like the guy was lifted up.'

'That will be Jona's decision. Let's make sure we get this right. Once you set up, you and I are going to sit down and start interviewing people. We need to get some names together, work out who was about. They said it was something to do with a muster, so I think we start off with the platform manager himself, get a brief overview of what went on. Let's get Jona set up.'

Macleod turned away from Hope when he saw David McCallan re-enter the kitchen. 'Mr McCallan, I need a word. Once I've got my forensic team set here, I want to see you in your office alone. You can run me through what you think happened starting from that muster you talked about.'

'Of course. Are we still able to use the kitchen? I need to feed all these people.'

'Ms. Nakamura will be in. She will cordon off areas. As long as your kitchen staff stay out of the way and follow whatever she says, they're good to go. If that means changing your menu, so be it. I'll meet you back in your office in ten minutes,' said Macleod. 'Be prepared to have everything with you with regards to what happened.'

'It's probably best if I bring in Andrea then as well,' said McCallan. 'She's my second here. She'll be able to bring in records of people working here, of course.'

'Of course,' said Macleod. 'Ten minutes.' He turned back to stare at the hanging cord in front of him.

It was ten minutes later that Macleod sat down in a seat opposite McCallan's desk. Hope was beside him and Andrea walked through the door carrying a multitude of files.

'May I introduce Andrea Roman, my deputy here on the platform.' Macleod stood and shook the woman's hand, followed by Hope, before they both sat down again.

'Do you have any coffee?' asked Hope. 'Frankly, I'm parched. I could really do with one.'

McCallan turned to Andrea, 'Get four.' The woman disappeared out of the room and Macleod suggested that they wait until she returned before starting. He turned to Hope and whispered in her ear, 'Thank you. I'm dry as a desert.' His partner smiled at him. She knew him too well, especially after the number of cases they had dealt with together.

Once the coffees had been established in front of them, Macleod opened his notebook, placed it on his knee, took a pen in hand, and gave a placid smile at David McCallan. 'In your own time, sir, just run through everything that happened, explaining what occurred and who did what.'

'Well, sir, I was in the bathroom, indisposed when the alarm for the muster went off. We found out afterwards it was a small fire on the other side of the platform.'

'Small fire?' said Hope, 'How did that go off?'

'Still working on it. We can't find anything electrical.'

'Possibly deliberate?' asked Hope.

'Unknown. It would surprise me knowing the people that work here but unknown.'

'Continue,' said Macleod.

'We got the call to muster, so I came back. Andrea and her team started checking off names and there was quite a few missing in the initial stages, but I'll let Andrea run through that. I placed a call to the mainland just to tell them something's going on. "We're checking if we have to shut down, making sure the systems are all running okay, prepared to put them into full closure if we have to." A team was sent out to check what the issue was. They found it was down to a small fire. They put it out. Andrea then came back to me and said, 'It's under control, but we've got a person missing.' By that stage, we've got everybody together.'

'How long from the initial muster call until that stage?' asked

Macleod.

'Twenty minutes. Yes, possibly twenty minutes.'

'How long were these people late in arriving? The ones you said didn't get there on time.'

'Andrea has a full list and she'll be able to have a rough idea when people arrived because she'll have that from questioning the other marshals at the muster station.'

'Okay, go on then, sir.'

'I sent a team to look for Angus. We knew at this point who was missing. Angus works in the canteen as a kitchen aide. The team proceeded that way and that's when they found him hanging in the kitchen. Andrea sent someone back for me. I went to find them there.'

'What did you do at that stage?' asked Hope.

'Well,' said McCallan, 'obviously, it's not a normal everyday situation. I kept everyone at muster for the next thirty minutes while we worked at what to do. We needed to get the rig running again. We made the call to say that somebody had died, but I wasn't sure— it looked like a possible suicide.'

'Bizarre time for a suicide,' said Hope. 'I thought you said his neck was badly broken before.'

'We did in the initial reporting and Andrea thought it was murder the whole time. I kind of hoped it wasn't, but we needed to get the oil going. We needed to get things operating again. People don't come out here quick. I knew there was going to be at least maybe twelve hours before someone arrived. You can't wait that long here. There are issues with the process, everything. We needed to keep going.'

'What did you do, sir?' asked Macleod.

'Well, we took him down and tried to preserve the body. We wrapped him up, put him in the cold store in the chiller.'

'Did you do anything else, anything that would assist the investigation instead of hindering it?' asked Macleod.

'Of course. Andrea took photos of everything. She insisted. She thought that was quite wise.'

'Are those available?' asked Macleod.

'Of course. Andrea, pass the inspector the photographs.' Andrea passed over the folder she brought in with her. Macleod opened it to see some A4 images.

'Where is the original camera that took these?' asked Macleod. 'We'll need that for evidence and the initials. Where were the initial photographs received? Those photographs are going nowhere. They come to us and they stay with us. Nobody publishes them anywhere. Is that understood?'

'Of course,' said McCallan. 'Who would want to publish them? Look at him hanging?'

Macleod looked down at the photograph in front of him. A black-haired man had his neck sitting to one side. 'That's so sharp an angle,' Macleod reckoned. 'It must've nearly snapped. He was hanging with his feet about three feet above the ground, electrical cord around his neck. Then at the back of the photograph, I can see where the cord was attached to the table leg.' Macleod shifted through the photographs and in truth, the deputy platform manager did a good job. She had taken photographs of the kitchen from various angles and closeups of all the main equipment that had been used in the murder.

'Do we know if Angus Macleod was in the kitchen when the muster alarm went off?'

'Yes,' said Andrea. He was in there with chef, all the kitchen staff.'

'What was he doing?' asked Macleod.

'Chef said he was chopping onions, but his body—' At this,

Andrea sniffed. 'His body didn't have his chef's outfit on. It was just a T-shirt he was wearing underneath.'

'If he was going to muster,' asked Hope, 'would he have taken that chef's top off?'

'He doesn't have to,' said Andrea. 'Maybe he might on the way out.'

'Did he leave before everyone else left?' asked Macleod.

'I don't know,' said McCallan. 'You're going to have to talk to people. We were busy. We were in the middle of a muster. We had the potential for the platform to be evacuated. We weren't thinking about where people were until they didn't turn up at the muster point.'

'All right,' said Macleod. 'In that case, I need to speak to everybody that works in the kitchen who was there at the time. I want anyone who was in the canteen as well. After that, we'll start speaking to everyone else, but I need to get an idea of who potentially was around and where Angus moved to when he left the kitchen. As you can imagine, this is going to take some time. I want you, Andrea, to sit with Hope, and I want you to go through the names of all your personnel and give them times for coming in to be interviewed by us. Hope will interview in one room. I'll interview in another. I want two rooms, McCallan, in which to do this.'

'Well, of course, inspector, we'll find something. It might not be that large, but we'll find something for you.'

'Also access to the Wi-Fi. I also want to start in two hours' time. You'll have to sort your shift times. I assume there'll be a certain number of people who were sleeping at that time. We'll see them last.'

'Two hours' time?' said McCallan. 'This is going to be hard to do. We got so many staff here. How long are you going to be interviewing them for.'

'That'd be five minutes. I don't want a queue. I'm not waiting for one after the other, so you need to sort this for me.'

'It can't be done,' said McCallan. 'It's crazy. I've got a platform to run.'

'Look, sunshine,' said Macleod, 'I don't care about your platform. If you want, I'll shut you down. I'll take everybody off here and we'll go and do it back in Shetland or Aberdeen or somewhere. If you want to avoid that, two hours' time, you've got your list ready and I'm starting to interview. Do you understand?'

McCallan nodded, but he was not happy. Macleod looked over at the deputy platform manager. She was screwing her face up. 'Is that achievable, Andrea?' he asked.

'I'll do my best, Inspector. Kitchen staff first, I'll go get on it. If you'd come this way, Detective McGrath.' With that, the women left to room.

'This isn't normal. You know that,' said McCallan.

'Murder's never normal. Nobody normally goes and murders anyone,' said Macleod. 'You've got somebody here and who's to say they won't do it again. The only reason your platform's still open is so I don't have them running off when they go back to the mainland. While they're here, they may think they're safe, but we'll see. Two hours, McCallan, that will be a late one.' Macleod stood up, walked out of the door closing it firmly behind him. He heard the word *tosser* as he made his way along the corridor. Macleod smiled.

Chapter 4

We haven't got overly long to do this,' said Macleod, 'so let's keep it as brief as we can. Detective McGrath and myself will be up to our eyeballs in interviews for the next day, so Ms Nakamura or Mr Corrin will have their work cut out trying to see if there's any piece of forensic evidence that hasn't been swept away or cleaned to oblivion in this place.'

Macleod had assembled his four-person team in his own quarters with the laptop set up on a video call back to the station in Inverness. The junior detectives on the team, Kirsten Stewart and Alan Ross, were sitting in on the call.

'Now, here's the state of play at the moment,' said Macleod. 'We know there was a call to muster on the station. We know that several people were late getting to the muster. We know that there was a fire set, possibly deliberate, possibly not. We're still working on that. That's what caused the muster. However, we also have one dead, Angus Macleod, kitchen staff and a resident of where, Kirsten?' asked Macleod.

'A resident of Stornoway, sir, Isle of Lewis. Several people on the rig come from over there. From what I can gather, he lives on his own, but that's just from electoral records and that.

I think I need to get over and do some ferreting around his house and amongst his friends, see what I can dig up.'

'That's an excellent idea. Are you okay to do it, though, with the way your brother is?'

'It's only Stornoway, sir. He's okay, and back out of the hospital. I think he'll be all right for a bit, so I'm happy enough to fly over in the morning to Lewis.'

'I'll hold the fort here,' said Ross. 'I take it you've got plenty more for me to get going through as well?'

'We're going to have to move the body back at some point. I dare say Jona will want a proper place to do her work as well. She'll get something temporary done, so that's going to require a lot of organization. Ross, we're going to have keep track of who's going to be coming on and off the rig. I want all manifests of passengers run through you, Ross. I want you to understand who's in, who's out on here, so that at any point if we have to go and get someone, you know where they are. I want addresses, Stewart, of all the rig workers as well. Until we can narrow down suspects, everyone here is a suspect.'

'When are they starting to take people off again and getting new arrivals?' asked Ross.

'They're intending to start it tomorrow,' said Hope, 'but we've insisted nobody leaves here until we've interviewed them, and we're going to put a stop on anyone going that we think has greater potential. It's going to take some mapping out.'

'I have already put some feelers out in Stornoway, sir. I spoke to the local constabulary,' said Stewart. 'They say our man, although he lives alone, is possibly part of the local model flying club. That seems a surprise because he lives in pretty much squalor. He's got a flat in Stornoway. That'll be my first port of call. The other thing to know about him is that in his bank account, there's a significant amount of money. That seems rather strange when he lives in squalor.'

'You say significant. What are you talking?' asked Macleod.

'From what I can gather, it's five figures at least, possibly touching six, very recently deposited in two transactions.'

'Do you know where they were deposited and when?' asked Hope.

'Still following up on it,' said Stewart. 'I'll have that detail by tomorrow.'

'Do we know if he was friends with anyone here?' asked Macleod.

'Not that I'm aware of,' said Hope, 'but we haven't spoken to anybody yet, but certainly, the platform manager and his deputy haven't put forward who Angus Macleod's friends were. To be honest, they didn't seem to know the guy that well. I guess they get so much traffic coming in and out of here, they can't know everybody. We'll probably get a better idea from the head chef. He'll be part of his staff, after all.'

'That's a good point,' said Macleod. 'We'd better be interviewing him early.'

'I'll get a run-through of the list of the people on the platform,' said Ross, 'and I'll see who else lives on the Isle of Lewis. It's quite possible that he's got a lot of friends from there. Maybe they work the rigs together. See if we've got people of a similar age.'

'Good idea,' said Macleod. 'Certainly, my people over there tend to stick together when they go away.' *My people,* thought Macleod. *It's a long time since I called them that.*

'That's a good line of attack, so let's start there. Identify his friends, both on the rig, off the rig. Get over to the flat. Find out if there was anything strange around there. Anything from you, Jona, so far?'

'Well, in terms of finding DNA and hairs or anything, the place is a mess,' said Jona. 'I'm going to be struggling to work anything out. He was definitely lifted up, but I think he was dead beforehand. I think his neck was broke separately and then he was put up there, maybe as an attempt to feign suicide, maybe as a way of showing punishment. I don't know. What I believe, without having had proper time to examine him, is that he was killed beforehand and then lifted up.'

'I take it that with a twenty-minute window, we can't be too exact about when it was that he died?' asked Macleod.

Jona raised her eyebrows. 'I'm afraid forensic science hasn't got that far advanced,' she said, 'and they've also stuck him in a fridge. Usually, if we get to within an hour or so, time-wise, we've done well, but you got a twenty-minute window, I thought. He was seen alive, wasn't he?'

'Yes,' said Macleod, 'that's what we've been told. I was just hoping forensic might be able to back that up.'

'Well, I've nothing to say anything different,' said Jona. 'I'll have a look and see what we can find out from him and from the body. In terms of putting him up there, it looks like they ripped down some of the wire from the ceiling, tied a bit round his neck, passed one up and over a hard beam, pulled him up with that wire, tying a wire to the leg.'

'Is there any way we can trace anybody to him, check under their fingernails and that?'

'I think they would have washed by now,' said Jona. 'Think how long has passed. Most people have been to the bathroom by now even if they were dumb enough not to have cleaned their hands up. I've got cooking grease in the air. The whole scene has just been contaminated. I'm not going to be able to get you much, Inspector. I'll do my best, but I think we're going to struggle. I also want to go over and have a look at the supposed fire and see what's caused that. Determining whether or not that was accidental or not could help the investigation.'

'If the fire was accidental, it's an incredibly opportune killing,' said Hope. 'To have the presence of mind to kill somebody that quickly, and then string them up, it looks more premeditated to me than the idea of stringing him up.'

'But why?' asked Macleod. 'Why would you string anybody up here? Look outside. You've got a whole sea to dump a body into. It must be hard to rescue somebody if they were overboard here, especially with no life jacket on. If you killed them already, unless you recover the body, nobody knows that. This seems a really strange way to stage a pretend suicide.'

'Maybe they got interrupted sir,' said Ross. 'Maybe somebody came in on them. Do we know if he got killed in the kitchen?'

'We suspect he left it,' said Macleod, 'so we don't know. He would then have to have come back or been brought back to the kitchen. Of course, if they are going to feign suicide, it's going to be in a place that identifies with Angus Macleod, which would be the kitchen. He really only would be between his quarters in the kitchen working here, or down to the gym facilities, or the other recreational things in the block, the accommodation block. I think it's time for us to gather things together. It's going to be a long slog, and I doubt that we're going to get much sleep over the next twenty-four hours, but nothing new there,' said Macleod. 'Well, Hope and myself over here have got every trust in you, Ross, and yourself, Kirsten. Get over to Lewis, take charge. Keep me updated about what's going on, but make sure you ferret out things. There's a lot of money involved in these oil rigs, and I am threatening to close them down if I have to, but in reality, we don't want to. It's just going to cause a lot of hassle, but we need to keep track of where people are going. Stay on top of this. It's very easy for this to get diluted with so many people here. We need to get an understanding of Angus Macleod quickly and his contacts even quicker. Once we can reduce the suspects, it'll be easier for us to manage them. Until then, there's no way I can restrict the movement of several hundred people.'

'If that's everything, sir, I'm just going to go and put in a bit of a running time before I sit down for the next twenty-four hours,' said Hope.

'A run?' said Macleod. 'When did you bring running gear with you?'

'It's in the bag. I always carry it in the boot. Running gear, anywhere we have to go, it's the grab bag. Don't you have one?' Macleod looked embarrassed.

'I don't have a grab bag. It sort of more gets provided for me,' said Macleod.

'You hit the jackpot with her, sir, didn't you?' laughed Hope.

Macleod feigned a little embarrassment in front of his team before building himself up again. 'Right. Joking aside, let's get to it. You check in with me later tonight, Ross. Kirsten, get home. Go see your brother. Get on the first flight over in the morning to Lewis. Jona, go and see about that fire. I agree with you. That's probably where we're going to find out more things forensically than anywhere else. Everyone, take care. We don't know what we're dealing with here. It's a murder, and until we understand the killer, watch your backs as ever.'

Macleod watched his team disappear from the room, leaving

37

just him sitting in front of a blank laptop. In half an hour, Hope and himself would be sitting down to interview people from the rig, asking their whereabouts, pushing to know what they had done, staring at their faces to work out if they were killers. He was already tired. After all, it was well into the evening and outside was dark.

Taking himself out of his room, he walked through the accommodation block until he got to the outside area, and he could stare at the sea from the gangway. The wind was reasonably calm, and he saw the sea gently roll up against the rig. Maybe that was a first; maybe out here it was a lot rougher, but now, it didn't seem like that bad a place to work. He seemed to understand the idea of dividing life up between work and pleasure. Three weeks, work your socks off. Three weeks, go and enjoy yourself. For three weeks, go and be a father. For three weeks, go and tour the world. He knew the pay was good here, probably better than what Macleod was earning, and they didn't have to deal with death and despair either. Well, at least normally, they didn't. McCallan was no doubt struggling to deal with it, as was Andrea Roman, and so was an entire population of a rig. Would they be nervous? Would they start distrusting each other? Would there be any unrest on the rig?

Macleod wondered if it would be wise to say that Angus Macleod had been killed, or should he call it an accident until people had left? But, of course, he could not do that. He was a police officer, after all. So, therefore, they were just treating the death as suspicious. Maybe that was not a good phrase either. Carrying out investigations, that was about it. Still, twenty-four hours and he had a whole rig of people to get through.

Chapter 5

Hope was sick of this room, sick to the core. It was bland, had no decorations on the walls and consisted of a small table with two plastic chairs, and a light, that would occasionally flicker. At three o'clock in the morning, the last thing she needed was a light messing with her eyes. They were having enough difficulty as it was.

She had gulped when she saw the list of employees that they would have to interview over the next twenty-four hours, and in fairness, most were done at pace. Given that the man had been in the kitchen and left it prior to being murdered, there was only a certain distance he could have travelled. The general consensus was he hadn't been seen on about 75% of the rig. The other 25%, which was mainly based around the accommodation area and the canteen, meant they could narrow the suspects down straight away. This, however, meant there were still a good number they had to get through.

The last suspect— or interviewee; after all, most of these people would have nothing to do with the murder— was a man with dark eyes. He simply stared at Hope. He was on his way back to the mainland in two days' time, and had a house on the outskirts of Aberdeen. He lived alone, and Hope deeply wanted to pin something on the man for the way he looked at her. He never said anything out of line, but his eyes gave it away. Yes, occasionally he did stare at her face, but not that often.

Regardless, she ran through where he was and what he had done and cross-referenced it with several other people who had mentioned him. He was not in the frame at all, and with that, she had got him packing back to his work, and out of her hair. It was not that she felt threatened. She could have taken the man apart in an instant. It was just, oh, he was just a sleaze ball.

Thankfully, most of her experience with the workers had been standard. Most felt a little nervous. After all, there had been a murder on the rig. Most were also extremely helpful, informative, and keen to clear their name.

The door opened and Andrea leaned in. 'You are ready for the next one?'

'No,' said Hope. 'If you don't mind, I think I'm going to have a break, and if it's possible, can I get some food? I'm absolutely starving.' The deputy platform manager nodded and closed the door leaving Hope with the flickering light bulb. 'Forget this,' she thought. 'I'm going outside for some air.' Opening the door, she saw a line of chairs in the corridor with six men sat there. 'I won't be long. I'll be back in a minute,' she said, and got a mixed response.

Some, no doubt, were happy that they didn't have to do any work at this point. Others were nervous that they were going to go into a police interview. Maybe they had never been interviewed before in their life. Frankly, Hope did not care, and she made the short journey outside onto the open gangway.

Outside, she could hear the waves crashing, but she struggled to see them. They were down there, and the lights of the rig allowed various shades of black to be seen. Again, the exact picture was difficult, especially with her tired eyes. Not that it mattered to her, as she breathed deeply, sucking in the air. She suddenly thought she should have brought a jacket with her, as the cool air struck her arms, but it was enlivening, picking her up.

We could be here for another four or five hours going through these names. That was the thing about Seoras— he was a taskmaster. If something needed done, there was never a question of whether you were up to it. It was just a case of, we get on with it, and we don't stop until we get to the end. How the man kept his mental wits about him at times like these, she didn't know. She knew she was jaded, and she thought back to twenty-four hours previous.

John Allen, the name ran through her mind. Suddenly, she remembered the first time she saw him, pitching up at his flat to ask about a suspect who had rented a car from him. Even then, she had been quite taken, and the man had been forward in a nice way. The way that says, 'I want to know you more,' not the one that says 'I'm God's gift to women.' *Complimentary, and there was nothing wrong with that*, thought Hope.

After a month of playing it cool and realizing that he was the genuine deal, they'd finally become intimate. Jona had been at Hope for the last month telling her that this guy was the one, but Hope wasn't sure if he was. One thing was for sure, he was probably going to be around for the next year at least. As long as she didn't screw it up. She had a track record of that.

No, she didn't. Seoras had called it. Had said they weren't worthy of her. Had said that they tried to make her something she wasn't, something the Inspector never did. Hope knew inside that she held the flame for him, and if he'd been twenty years younger, she might even have acted on it. When she first met Seoras, he was broken and maybe she had helped heal him in some way, but they had made such a good team, building up their little unit.

Although she still saw him as the Inspector, the senior, the man she could learn off, that little flame had never left. She wondered how many people carry these flames. Lights that would burn bright but would never be acted on because the circumstances were wrong, because their ages were wrong, because life was wrong.

Hope nearly jumped out of her skin a hand touched her shoulder.

'Any luck?'

'You once told me it was not about luck', said Hope. 'It's was all about thorough detection, all about chasing the culprit down. Luck doesn't come into it.

'Of course, luck comes into it,' said Seoras, 'but are you okay? Do you want to call it a night? You can get some sleep if you want, come back in about four hours. I'll carry on,' he said.

'What? Leave you here? We've got to let them think they've got a chance'

'A chance? What do you mean, a chance?'

'A chance to see the good-looking one,' said Hope, 'instead of Mr Grumpy.' She watched his eyes, moving in that way that scanned her expression. Once he realized it was a joke, he gave a slight shrug of shoulders. That was the thing about Seoras—he didn't always catch the joke, first time.

'Why didn't they just bring him out to somewhere like this?' asked Macleod. 'Why not just toss him over the side? Chances are we wouldn't even be here. The body would never be found, just a happy accident.'

'Maybe they couldn't get him out. I'm amazed how many people are milling about here. Have you discounted much of your list?'

'Most of it,' said Seoras. 'Thankfully, most of it's pretty monotonous though. You get a sense that most of them are shocked.'

'Only to a point,' said Hope. 'From some of them, I get the feeling that their attention is here on the rig. From some of them, I get the feeling that maybe they expected something, but not this far, not like this.'

'It's very brutal. I'll give you that,' said Seoras. 'Jona came in to see me an hour ago. She's really struggling to pick up anything, any prints, any DNA. The trouble is that most people can be through there. She said that the chef reckoned that several people pass through the kitchen. He often requests help with moving things and then the wire itself had no prints on it. Jona said it was clean, like somebody had used gloves.'

'Has she gotten anywhere on the fire?'

'She said it was highly likely it was deliberate. The problem is it's very hard to prove it completely. There's very little that could accidentally have gone wrong with it. The area is burnt; it's gone through some electrical wires, so the possible cause could have vanished in the fire and as Jona says, "She's not an expert in this field." She's talking about trying to get someone out, a fire officer. Someone who understands the ins and outs of rigs as well. The staff here on the rig are saying that it definitely wasn't a malfunction. They can't find any evidence of it and I'm inclined to believe that. If was set deliberately, then there must have been a plan.'

'Certainly a plan to get to Angus Macleod, send everyone scattering,' said Hope. 'Whether or not they meant to kill him in the kitchen is another matter. It seems very ad hoc, very quick to grab the wire; surely they'd have to have things ready and he'd need to have left and come back. Several of my suspects had seen Angus once he left the kitchen. Fortunately, most of them have got alibis, reducing the number. There's only one or two who said they saw him but we can't confirm that they didn't do anything to him. They were alone when they spotted him.

'They were interrupted, Hope. They had to be interrupted in what they were doing. If the plan came that they set the fire to get everybody moving then they would expect Angus to go to muster. They've intercepted him but he's not been where they wanted him to be. Therefore, they had to dispatch him quickly and they made it look like suicide so there was no intention to let anybody know he had been murdered. I still think they were going to shove him off the side here. Look down there.'

Hope leaned over the railing down towards the darkness below. The occasional white spray hit the rig and the bright lights showed the churning sea.

'No life jacket on, I reckon you'll be lucky to get twenty minutes in there' said Macleod. 'I know the survival tables say better, but you'll hit the water, you'll be cold, you'll panic. That will start to take you down. Once you go under, you're not going to just float back up. You need to have the presence of mind to hit the water, then lie and relax to float, hoping that somebody knows you're missing. If everyone mustered, you could just throw somebody in on the far side, and no one would see them. If you've given them a good dig to the head, you can knock them out and they'll just disappear straight into the drink forever. I say we're looking for an interruption, Hope.'

'Have you got anywhere with finding out who his friends are?'

'I'm getting the impression he's quite a loner. Certainly not many. All Lewis boys. That's who he spoke to.'

'They said there's quite a clique from Lewis. Certainly, in those smaller groups. I'll be interested to see how many of them we can relate to him.'

'Indeed, but let's not get fixated. Stewart should be over there in the morning. We'll get her to run the names of the clique as well. See if anybody over there knows if they hung about together.'

'Excuse me, Inspector, Detective,' interrupted Andrea Romain,' I was just wondering if you were going to be coming back in. We need to get through these people. They need to be back on shift. It's quite tight number-wise on the platform. If you take people out, it gets awkward to keep things running. I know we said we'll cooperate as best we can but you need to understand we've got our demands here as well.'

'What would you do if one of them was sick?' asked Macleod. 'This is a murder investigation. I'll be ready when I'm ready, as will Sergeant McGrath. Until then, they can wait in the corridor.

Andrea, the deputy platform manager nodded sheepishly, as if rebuked and Hope turned to her, 'Thanks for your assistance.'

'You need to keep them on their toes,' said Seoras, watching Andrea return inside. 'They'll tell you they need to do this, they need to do that. What they don't want is us uncovering things but that's exactly what we need to do. We need to get to

45

the core of what's going on in here. I mean it should be simple. You fly out, you do your work, you go home but there won't be, there'll be little communities here. They're all groups and cliques, tensions. Remember you've also got a lot of men here away from home. Three weeks, that's a long time. Long time without any intimacy. Men aren't good without intimacy.'

'If you say so, Seoras.'

'I do say so; we're not. Before Jane, I was rubbish, I was snappy, really grumpy. Taking everything out on people in my work.'

'Now you're the life and soul of the party.'

'Now I'm a lot better, as will you be.'

Hope raised her eyebrows at him, 'I don't know what you're referring to.'

'Come on, Hope. If we're honest, you've struggled ever since you came up, all you've wanted is that close person. John has been very good for you Don't get me wrong, but you want more; maybe you found it. I hope so, I really do.'

Hope suddenly smiled. 'We best get back before we bring the rig to a standstill, with all our gassing in those rooms.'

'Indeed. But I'll lose it if the coffee runs out or that light flickers again.' Macleod gave Hope a fierce stare.

'It'll be best to get you back to Jane then. Looks like the angst is growing again already.'

Chapter 6

Kirsten Stewart was not having a good morning. First, she'd had to leave her brother at the care home. He'd had a short stay in the hospital and was now back in a temporary respite. In previous years, Kirsten had always been assisted by extra help coming along throughout the day or by dropping her brother into his club for adults with special needs, but the illness had become worse, causing him to have an attack, and now he needed to be observed for twenty-four hours at least, possibly longer.

With her job, there was no way Kirsten could be with him and her brother had been taken into care. It was the best place for him, but it marked a worrying trend over the last year of incidents. With no other family, Kirsten had been the sole carer for a long time for her brother. She always knew that the possibility of him having to be taken into state care was there but it was something she had tried not to think about.

With recent approaches made to her by those in the intelligence services looking to recruit her, family life had been occupying her mind a lot. How would her brother cope if she changed jobs? He seemed to like Inverness; he seemed to like the area. Whenever she took him out either for walks or just simply to see the scenery and the shops, he seemed at peace but his health was failing, and pretty soon, she wouldn't be able to cope with him. It was coming; the only thing she did not know was exactly when.

After catching her flight from Inverness to Stornoway, Kirsten briefly dropped by the Stornoway station to announce her intentions. It was a courtesy call just in case they got any reports of someone snooping around, for that was her purpose here, to snoop, to find out all about Angus Macleod. Taking a hire car, Kirsten made her way out to an estate on the edge of Stornoway. It looked fairly rough but certainly nothing to what she'd seen in Inverness.

There were several interlinking courtyards, houses shoved together in rows. Occasionally, some of them were flats. *Social housing at its finest*, she thought. *Why do they always look like the drabbest areas? The walls were that rather pale colour. In Scotland, you knew the weather was not going to be wonderful for most of the year, why didn't they make the houses brighter? There was that place down in the Isle of Mull, Tobermory, with a bright front by the sea. Maybe they should do their houses like that*, Kirsten thought, as she parked up the car and made sure she locked it behind her.

The crime rate in Lewis was not high. Maybe it was just that feeling of not knowing where you were. Stewart had been here; she'd served six months on Lewis before being recruited by Macleod, so the place was not completely new to her. Glancing at a piece of paper, she made her way to the flat of Angus Macleod which started with a door in a wall between two other flats. His was upstairs, and Stewart wondered the best way to get in.

As she approached the front door, she was surprised to see

it half-open. Slowly, she approached, listening, trying to hear if anyone was inside. When nothing was heard, she rapped the door with her hand. 'Police, anyone inside. This is the police, please identify yourself.'

On hearing no sound, Stewart stepped inside, closing the door behind her. She saw that the lock had been broken, smashed through from the wood, but there was a chain, and she attached it to make sure the door would not open far. Beneath her feet were a few bills and other letters. Stewart lifted them, stacking them carefully to one side. Slowly, she walked up the blue carpeted stairs, noting that the carpet was threadbare on several of the steps, more than needing replacement.

As she reached the top of the stairs, Stewart approached a large lounge with a TV on the far side that dominated the room. Several bottles of liquor were on a sideboard, and there were still crisps on the floor. *The man lives like some sort of pig*, thought Stewart. She made her way through the room, to a small kitchen unit at the rear. The fridge was bare except for a few cans and some butter. While not having been tidied away, the kitchen was certainly clean, not somewhere you would expect to see mice.

She made a quick check through all of the cupboards. There were more bills stacked up at the side of the kitchen sideboard. Running her way through them, Stewart noted a number in arrears. There was a lack of photographs as Stewart made her way through to the bedroom of the small flat where there was a double bed.

On opening the wardrobe, she found many modern clothes, some thrown in a pile at the bottom of the wardrobe, clearly ready for washing next time the owner returned. But she also saw a small box at the bottom of the wardrobe with a lock on it. The lock was a mere padlock, small, requiring a key. There was a table beside the bed and on opening the small drawer in the table, Stewart located a key that seemed to be about the right size. She undid the padlock, putting it to one side, throwing back the lid of the small box.

There were a number of DVDs inside as well as some magazines. Taking them out, she realized the sort of magazines they were and replaced them in the box carefully. *Obviously, a single man*, she thought. Stewart checked the DVDs from the box which were unmarked. She placed one of them inside a DVD recorder attached to the TV. Within thirty seconds of watching the first one, she decided that they needed to be put back. Stewart was not shocked by a lot but certainly, these things in front of her were graphic and of a bedroom nature.

Returning to the lounge, Stewart looked around at the drab curtains and the overall lack of effort in the place. Clearly the guy didn't get a lot of kicks and what he did were coming from the box. There were several ordinary DVDs sat beside the TV, blockbuster movies and the sort, but everything just said here was a person who vegged out. On opening more cupboards, Stewart located yet more booze and the picture of Angus Macleod seemed complete. *Why kill him?* thought Stewart. *It seems very bizarre.*

She made her way back down the stairs, unhooking the door and exiting. Taking some tape from the car, she crossed a couple of strands from her POLICE AWARE roll over the front door, much to the amusement of some kids behind her.

'We could still get in there,' said a chirpy lad. He could not have been more than about nine years old.

'But you won't, will you?' said Stewart. 'Because if you do, we'll have to come and take you away.'

'How are you going to know if we're in there? Besides, it's only booze.'

'Have you been in?' asked Stewart.

'Well, you have, haven't you? If you've been in, why shouldn't I?'

'Because I'm the police,' said Stewart. 'It's my job. You're not meant to be in there. Did you know who owns it?'

'Angus. Angus lives in there. He works on the rig. He's away at the moment,' said the child. The kid had brown hair cut in that traditional bowl that you get before you think about styling it. He was grinning from tooth to tooth at the thought he had been inside, somewhere the police were trying to keep people out of.

'What do you know about him other than he works in an oil rig?'

'I don't know much. I never went in there when he was home. We went in the other day. There were some cans about.'

'Did you take any?' asked Stewart. The boy looked nervous. 'It's okay. You can tell me. I just need to know what you've touched in there so we can rule you out from any investigation.'

That wasn't completely true but Stewart hoped that the boy would start to talk. It worked. 'We didn't break the door down. We didn't kick it in. That wasn't us.'

'Do you know who it was?' asked Stewart.

'Yes. There was a guy who's been hanging about all the time.

'All the time?' queried Stewart. 'How long's all the time?'

'Last two weeks. Since the Old Firm derby, Rangers-Celtic match. It's just after that. I think that's two weeks.'

Stewart tried to do the calculation in her head. Her brother liked to watch the Old Firm games. Yes, it was. It was two weeks. 'What did this guy look like?' asked Stewart.

'It's a bit strange. He always wore glasses. Sometimes they were sunglasses. Sometimes they were ordinary glasses. Always glasses on. He used to come knock the door. We hid because he looked scary.'

'Was he bigger than me?' asked Stewart.

'No offense but everybody is bigger than you.'

'Well, you're not,' said Stewart.

'No, but I'm a kid. All the adults are bigger than you.'

'So how much bigger than me?' asked Stewart.

'Well, maybe this much,' Stewart looked at the kid's hands. *So, another what, foot? He'd be around about six foot.* 'Did you see him when he went inside the day he broke the door?'

'Oh, yes. We were over there behind the cars just so he didn't see us. He always moved away when he saw people.'

'Did you see him come out with anything?' asked Stewart. 'From the house?'

'No, but he looked really angry. Very annoyed. I don't know why. Nobody else was in there. We went in afterward but nobody else saw him. Only us, and he didn't see us because we were hiding really well.'

'He just left the door like that?'

'Yes. It's been like that for a couple of days now.'

Stewart noticed a woman opening a door from one of the houses across the square. She raced over quickly. The woman was still in her slippers and some jeans and a pink jumper on. Her hair was not brushed.

'Are they bothering you?' asked the woman.

'No. They're not. They're being very helpful.' With that, Stewart produced a warrant card. 'I'm DC Stewart and this house behind me is being investigated. Are these your children?' asked Stewart.

'The one at the front is,' said the woman. 'I'm Daniela MacIver. That's my son, Mark.'

'Well, Mark's been telling me about a man who's been seen around here. Have you seen anything at all?'

'Oh, that guy. Mark told me. I told him to stay away from him. It sounded a bit like trouble.'

'Did you know Angus?'

'Know as in past tense?' said the woman. 'What's happened to him?'

'I'm afraid there's been an incident on the oil rig that Angus works on. He won't be coming home,' said Stewart trying not to say anything too dramatic in front of the children. The neighbour nodded.

'Do you think this man had anything to do with it?'

'I'm just carrying out routine investigations,' said Stewart. 'How long since the man has been about?'

'About two weeks,' said the woman.

'That's what I told her,' said Mark.

'Yes, you did,' said Stewart. 'Yes, you did. But sometimes we all get confused so I just like to have two people say it to me. If you kids can just move on a wee bit, I need to talk to your mum, Mark. Is that okay?' The boy was shooed away by his mum. She stood with her arms folded looking at Stewart.

'You said there was an incident. What do you mean an incident?'

'We believe he was possibly killed illegally. We're just running investigations to find out if that was the case. Can you tell me anything about Angus?'

'He was a bit of a lost soul really. Kept himself to himself in there. Didn't go out much.'

'Did he go anywhere?' asked Stewart.

'Well, yes, he was part of the Model Flying Club. That's true. If he did go out for a drink, he would have gone down to the South Beach Bar. It's the one down in town, not very reputable.'

'Don't worry, I'm well aware of the South Beach Bar,' said Stewart, remembering having to drag several people out of it during her previous duties on the island.

'Other than that, that was it. The bar occasionally on a Saturday night, maybe once during the week, and the Model Flying Club. Spent a lot of time in his own flat alone.'

'Was he lonely?'

'Very. There was a group of them that used to hang about. I don't know all their names. I think he still saw some of them. I'm not sure. Angus was very self-contained. He didn't like a lot of attention. He got very embarrassed one day. There was a big box delivered for him, left outside the house. Some of the kids here opened it up because he had not come down and collected it. Well, it was things of an adult nature, magazines, and things as well. Of course, the kids are having a field day with this but Angus had to come down and collect in front of everyone. He wasn't best pleased.

'I felt for him, I have to be honest, officer. I felt for him. He was just a lonely guy on his own. I'm not sure what influence his parents had on him. Can't remember him ever being in trouble or hearing about them on the island but clearly, he wasn't very outgoing. He never got over that adolescent thing that boys have.'

'How do you mean?' asked Stewart.

'Well, maybe it's the mother thing but sometimes they look at you as if— well, sizing you up shall we say. Not as a person, as an object. Off to some dreams,' the woman laughed. 'Guess

I'm going to get issues like that with my boys growing up. All normal. I'm not saying he was doing anything that wasn't normal but I don't think Angus got past his adolescent stage.'

'He wasn't that long out of it. I understand that he was only twenty-five,' said Stewart.

'Yes, he was quite young but that's about it. I don't know much else about him. As I said he stayed in that flat.'

'Thank you for that,' said Stewart. 'They'll be some officers coming up and securing the door. Your Mark has been in the house. I believe he's probably taking some cans and stuff. I'm not interested in that as a police matter but there's more possibly going to come from this flat. There may be forensic people coming in, so Mark needs to stay away. I don't want him to get into trouble.'

'I don't want him seeing any of that stuff that Angus had. Okay, I'll get hold of him. Don't you worry.' With that, the woman started shouting at the top of her voice, 'Mark. Mark. Get here.'

Stewart almost laughed and got into her car. She'd call the station and get them to send someone up to make sure the building was secured but really, she needed to go and see the Model Club. Picking up her phone, Stewart googled the Stornoway Model Flying Club and got a contact for the chairman. When she googled his name, she realized he worked at the council, and decided to make her way there for a more discreet inquiry than phoning ahead.

Men's magazines. Model Club Flying. Do they go hand-in-hand? she thought. *Maybe I should ask the boss.* With that, she burst into a fit of giggles.

Chapter 7

Macleod was impressed with the food, expecting something similar to the 1970s or a roadside cafe. He found instead that the quality, as well as the quantity, was excellent. Although it must have been hard to cook with Jona running around inside the kitchen, telling the chef you can't do this and you can't do that, the end results belied any notion that the cooking was somehow inferior; the large lumps of steak and the pie in front of him, with a rather excellent gravy and puff pastry, helped to lift Macleod's mood. After interviewing for what seemed like forever and a day, he was approaching the end of his interviewees. Progress had been made and at the moment it looked like they were able to narrow down numbers. There were maybe only twenty or so who could have committed the killing. He wasn't sure as they were still cross-checking and running things through Ross who was then entering names and finding out about the people and their lives on the mainland. But Macleod was sure that the number was becoming manageable.

'Sorry to bother you, Inspector, but you did say you wanted to be updated.'

Macleod looked up into the face of Jona Nakamura, the

diminutive, but quite brilliant Asian forensic investigator. 'Take a seat,' he said, 'it's fairly quiet here. Unless you've got something that's very sensitive to tell me, I'm sure we can keep a reasonable level of conversation that won't be eavesdropped on.'

Jona sat down and Macleod saw that the woman had a full cup. The sweet smell of raspberry was emanating from it. *It must be one of those infusions. Quite modern-day really* thought Macleod. When he'd started out in the police force, if somebody had brought a cup of hot water filled with raspberries, strawberries and citrus fruits, a few eyebrows would have been raised, a few comments said that certainly would not have been PC. These days if you didn't have some personal type of drink, you were seen as being old hat. *Whatever,* thought Macleod, *a decent cup of coffee is all I need wherever I am.* With that, he lifted his own cup to his lips and drank the hot liquid. *Yes, a decent cup of coffee is all you need. But this is only half-decent.* Placing the cup back down, he smiled at Jona, opening his hands to indicate he was ready to listen.

'I'm not sure we're going to be able to work this out simply on the location of the attacker or by finding DNA at the scene. There's a high risk of cross-contamination because they moved the body and also because they've had a working kitchen around it. I can tell you something. Whoever pulled the wiring, cleaned it, either that or they wore gloves. Now I'd go with this idea of cleaning because there's nothing on the wire, nothing at all. Now, when the wiring was installed, you might've got some partial print on the wire because obviously, it's a very small surface area, but it looks to me like it's been cleaned thoroughly. Of course, it could just be time. After all, prints don't last forever. I think whoever hanged Angus Macleod certainly knew what they were about.'

'You said whoever hanged Angus Macleod. Do you think somebody else killed him?'

'I have no idea,' said Jona. 'Again, I'm struggling for any marks on the victim. I'd like to get back to a proper lab with the body and do some more thorough research on it. With what I've got here, from what I can do and given the fact that they threw him into a cold chill, I'm left with a number of fingerprints on his clothing. Now everyone that put the body into that chill— I referenced the platform manager to find out who did that— their fingerprints are on him. Nobody else's, just theirs. I found a couple of hairs as well but again, they belong to those who carried him in and I've got nothing from anyone else. I did take a run through the witness statements. I believe that I can guess that Angus Macleod on hearing the alarm, left the kitchen. He was then seen in several corridors outside. I've got his handprint on several of them, but he's been here for how long? Several weeks. Then he's not seen. I did check the body though. He was definitely dead before he was hanged.'

'The break on the neck was terminal?' asked Macleod.

'Oh yes,' said Jona, 'definitely. I guarantee that he was dead before they lifted him up. Just the whole way the neck is marked from the cord. That's a dead body pulled up. There's also no struggle.'

'Do you know why they killed him though?' asked Macleod. 'And why's it in the kitchen? Although that's only a guess from the photographs when they found him. He's hanging, there's no disturbance. If this wasn't a premeditated attack, the alarm's going off, he's going to do something with him, just kill him, and then hang him in the canteen instead of simply stepping outside and throwing the body overboard. You'd expect a live body or somebody, if he isn't quite dead, to be struggling and kicking out. You'd find a mess in the kitchen. That's not the case. Their photographs prove that. Unless it's a hell of a coverup where they put everything back in the photographs. To my mind, he's dead when he goes up there.

'My idea is that it's been bungled; that they've rushed to do it in the kitchen. It's just a theory I've got. It just seems crazy to me that you wouldn't just chuck somebody over the side? What about the fire? What did you find out about it?'

'Definitely done on purpose,' said Jona. 'I've had a look at the electrical wiring, and I can't see how that's happened by accident. Somebody set a fire there. I'm still struggling to find what ignited it. Maybe they took that away with them. There's plenty of hot works gear around here, although they're pretty strict about how you move it about. There are certainly enough things that are flammable. Look at the burn marks in the area. It looks like someone sprayed something on the wall around the electrical unit and set fire to it. That would be my guess.'

'So, we can search,' said Macleod, 'for sources of ignition fuel, canister sprays, things that are likely to go up when a match is stuck to them, that sort of thing. Is that right?'

'You could search; it's been how long? Must be coming up to nearly two days now. We're right here in the ocean. It's the easiest thing to throw it over the side. Nobody's going down there to have a look, especially something that may be a can. I mean what amount of fuel would be needed to start a fire like that. Looking at it, the fuel could have been stored inside of a deodorant can.'

'Do we have anything on the platform that can actually be

used for that?'

'They wouldn't have to bring it on with them. I assume that when you come in a helicopter to here, you're not going to be able to take anything of that nature. Supply ships should be bringing that sort of stuff onboard. I'd agree with that. It'd be hard to smuggle, to sneak on board. They've got enough stuff here that could be an ignition source, sprays and tins of different things. It wouldn't be hard to make one nor to find one I would reckon.'

'Do you think you'll ever find the ignition source properly, be able to name it for me?'

Jona shook her head. 'It's almost getting too long, now. I'm taking samples and that, but I'm going to struggle with that one, if I'm honest.'

'So, what do we have,' asked Macleod. 'We have Angus Macleod in the canteen. We have a call to muster that comes about because of a deliberately set fire. Somebody is going to get from that fire over to the kitchen area and accommodation block. They've got to then grab Angus on his way past, kill him without anybody seeing, drag him back into the kitchen, hang him. The last part I can see but what about the first bit? It's a fair run across. Could they have set the fire in such a way that it takes time to really ignite?'

'I spoke to the platform manager, David McCallan, and according to him, it is a good hike from there across to the accommodation block. They've got to set the fire and then got to shift it,' said Jona. 'However, I also didn't find any remote ignition. I believe at the time, somebody must've been there to light it. That means that the area it was set in would have to be fairly remote, not used that often. You're looking at sensors, picking it up as opposed to people.'

'Did you ask Mr McCallan about that?'

'Of course,' said Jona. 'He said, it's quite a remote part of the station. There wouldn't be that many people passing through. It's also what makes me think it's deliberate. It's very clever, giving them time to move all that way.'

'Also, I guess, Macleod is on the move and he's had a call to muster, so he's not going to stop for anyone. Is he? Unless it's a friend? Unless it's somebody he knows. Maybe they call to him saying, "Give us a hand with this" or whatever or "take this to the room."'

'As it's a muster call,' said Jona, 'you wouldn't stop for anything.'

'You say that. But people do; people will stop for things. Stop for a packet of something. Maybe they've got something important. Maybe they've got drugs on board, or he knows something. You can always find a reason that somebody will stop, especially if he knew them well. I've also been thinking about the killer, or maybe killers. They're going to be fairly strong because they're going to kill him and take him to the kitchen— although I still believe the original plan was to kill him, take him outside, and launch him over the side. I looked at the accommodation block, looked at how you come out of the kitchen. Then Angus is on his way coming out of the kitchen towards the muster point, which is more towards the front-end of the accommodation block. If he gets attacked quite close in, they can take him back to the corridor that leads to the outside gangway, and you could chuck him off from there. The problem is if somebody else is still out there, in that direction. You have to do what you need to do, or he comes into your room and you do what you need to do. Then you can't just hang on to him. If somebody is blocking the way, if somebody's blocking that exit because they're still messing about to get to the call to muster then he takes a route back to the kitchen because he knows that's going to clear quick, people leaving their food. Mr McCallan told me that when the muster call activates, the kitchens kill all the electricity. Everything dies down.'

'Maybe that's why they were okay to cut the wire,' said Jona.

'I'll finish the interviews, Jona, and then I'm going to bring you, McGrath and myself together. You can bring in Alan as well if you wish. We'll get a full link up to Ross, maybe Stewart will join us. We'll sit down and work out who could be involved. Then we go hard at those people, at their life land side, whatever link can be made to Angus Macleod as well. I think we're going to get in the twentiess or thirties, the number of people who could potentially have done this. It'll be quite handy if we can actually find some tangible evidence towards them, but you're pretty confident that's never going to happen, aren't you?

'I doubt it. it's not like I'm not trying,' said Jona. 'It's just so messed up. This is not a clean crime scene I walked into. This is an absolute mess and I'd tell you to shut it down, just kill the platform, except it's not going to do any good. They had already moved the body. They'd already contaminated the scene. There's so little left for me.'

Macleod nodded his thanks to Jona and watched her pick up her cup, draining the last bit of hot liquid before placing it on a tray at the side of the canteen. When she left, he turned back and looked down at the table, his shoulders suddenly feeling heavy. The interviewing process had taken so long as there were so many people. There was nothing really to learn, but you still had to be polite. You still had to be sharp and on the lookout, just in case somebody said something or dropped something which blew your case wide open. Macleod felt a knot near the top of his shoulders and tried to wriggle them to take it away but then a pair of hands were suddenly on his shoulders, squeezing them gently.

'You know we haven't sat down and done any of the meditation we needed to do,' said Jona. At times in the past year, Macleod and Jona had taken time aside as he followed Jona's method of relaxation and of rebuilding the soul, as she put it. Purging was important with what they saw and with the hours that they put in, but right now he was struggling to stop his face from smiling too much as she worked her magic on his shoulders. He really needed to get Jona to teach Jane how to do this.

'We have missed and I've missed it,' he said. 'As soon as we get back, let's put some dates in the diary. It was a big help to me before. I'm sure it will be a big help for me again. Thank you, Jona, for thinking of it. It's very kind of you.'

'No, Seoras, it's very selfish. I've missed it too. You're quite a good wall to bounce things off and one that sits quite comfortably, if there's nothing to talk about. I've missed my quiet time partner so don't you worry, I'll make sure you put the time in the diary.'

With that, she worked his shoulders a little more before departing. Macleod looked up and four tables across from him, a worker was smiling. The man was tall and broad and he seemed to be giving Macleod a face that said, 'Certainly in there, sir.' At first, Macleod grinned and then he looked up and simply shook his head. The man opposite smiled, drunk the last of his tea, and walked off.

Not something that really should have been shown in public, felt

Macleod. *Not really a very good image for the department* and then the pain came back across his shoulders and he looked around. *I need a meditation room in the department.*

Chapter 8

Kirsten Stewart put down the phone. It seemed things were not so good for her brother, but at least he had slept well. Moving into fulltime care with other people, moving out of his house and into a place of supposed sanctuary and security had not appealed to him, but Kirsten knew it was the right thing to do. He needed 24/7 attention now and she couldn't give it to him as much as she'd pop in and see him whenever she could. In truth, he'd started to recognize her less and less. Whatever it was with his mind, whatever was happening to it, whatever form of dementia they called it, it was making her lose touch with him. She pulled back a tear, sniffed, and then looked out of the car window.

The car park at the football field was rather bland, basically a load of stones through which the reeds were poking. Over on the football pitch, there were a lot of grown men standing around talking and some carrying large toy planes under their arms. Stewart was a little bit bemused by this fascination with what she considered to be toys, but she needed the help of these people and so she was determined not to offend them. The day was fairly windy which she knew was not unusual for the Outer Hebrides and from her time here, she could recall a flying club, but it was just a name on a poster somewhere. She had never actually seen them in action. As she stepped out on to the football pitch, she looked up watching several planes circle around it. Maybe, they were one hundred, two hundred feet up. She couldn't be sure, but as she strode across the field she became fascinated watching one twist and turn.

'Get off the runway. Get off the runway.'

Kirsten looked around her. She couldn't see any runway. There was just grass. Then she stared ahead of her and saw a man waving at her furiously.

'Get back. Get off the runway. Abort. Abort it.'

Kirsten stepped backwards as the man ran forwards, and then another man began to wave his arms shouting before Kirsten saw the aircraft shoot just over the head of the saviour running towards her.

'What are you doing?'

'DC Kirsten Stewart, I need to speak to you, gentlemen. Can we find somewhere safe?'

'Follow me. We just need to go over there off the runway. Can't you see the runway?'

Kirsten looked left and right. There didn't seem to be anything. Oh, there were a couple of cones at the far end. 'Sorry,' said Kirsten. 'I'm afraid it's not my thing flying toys around like this.'

'Toys? They are not toys,' said the man, half jogging off the runway. 'These are delicately controlled models. They cost a small fortune to build and upkeep. It takes quite a dab hand to know what you're doing with them.'

'I stand corrected,' said Kirsten. 'My apologies.'

'Anyway,' said the man, 'You said you needed to speak to us. I'm the chairman, so what is it you need to know?'

'Oh, you're the chairman,' said Kirsten. 'You're probably the man then. I believe you're part of the council?'

'That's correct. Yes. My name's Donny. Donny Owens. Been a council member for the last eight years and also chairman of this club. Welcome to the Isle of Lewis Model Flying Club. As long as you keep off our runway, you're most welcome.'

Kirsten almost laughed and the man seemed friendly enough. He was rather squat, maybe about five foot six, not much taller than Kirsten herself. As she pushed her glasses back onto her nose, she saw him grin wildly. *Maybe they didn't get visitors here. Maybe they didn't get female visitors*, she thought. *Blimey, it's not going to be one of those conversations, is it?*

'Well, I'm sorry to bother you, sir, at this time, but I'm investigating a case in which the name of Angus Macleod has come up.'

'Angus Macleod, rather a common name around here, if you catch my drift.'

'Of course, it is, sir,' said Kirsten, 'This Angus Macleod was a flyer of model aircraft, as I believe. I've been told he was a member of your club, visited quite regularly. I was just trying to find out a little bit about him'

Over Donny's shoulder a man shouted, 'What's she wanting? What's the matter?'

'She wants to know about Angus Macleod. I'm just going to have a little word.'

'That little shit. Well, he's not welcome here. You can tell her that. He's not welcome here. We fly models here, not drones.'

'I take it he was quite a fractious character,' said Kirsten.

'Rather,' said Donny. 'You see, we're a model flying club. If you look out there, we've got all different types of model aircraft. Some petrol driven. Some battery driven, various types. Various materials, but they're all aircraft of some sort, so in real life you could see these being, you know, flown around large scale, pilots inside. We make models, smaller models, obviously, of these aircraft and we fly them.'

'Did Angus not do that?'

'Angus Macleod came along and said he wanted to fly his model. He then took out what was a rather large drone.'

'Is a drone not a model?' asked Kirsten.

'No,' said Donny. 'Forgive me, but it's like this; you don't have a large drone. You don't fly large drones around. A drone is a small aircraft that has nobody in it. We're flying models of real aircraft with people in them, so a drone isn't. It's got four propellers. It moves this way and that. You control it completely differently. It's not even a model aircraft, for goodness sake.'

Kirsten could feel Donny getting worked up. 'I'm sorry, I don't mean to upset you,' said Kirsten. 'I'm just pretty ignorant on this. A drone isn't a model aircraft— it's actually an aircraft?'

'That's correct. It's not a model. It's not a reduced scale. It's just an aircraft that's not got a pilot. If you look over there, Martin has got a helicopter, but it's a small helicopter, a model helicopter. The only pilot inside it doesn't move or turn his head. He's made of plastic.'

'I'm with you now, sir,' said Kirsten. 'Angus brought his drone. What did you say to him? Did you refuse him permission to fly?'

'You better come with me,' said Donny. 'There's too many ears around here. I don't want things to kick off. We're having rather a good day today.'

Kirsten nodded and followed Donny across the remainder of the football pitch and over to a small hut. In her mind she was wondering just exactly what could kick off at a model aircraft club. 'Just come in,' said Donny. 'Sit yourself down there on the bench. Do you take tea?'

'We usually have coffee, if I'm honest, but whatever you've got.'

'Well, I've got tea, so it's tea it's going to be,' said Donny. 'Right. Now, the kettle's on, so what I'll do is I'll take you through what happened. You see, Angus came along with the drone, and like I said, it was a big drone. The thing about that was some of the boys at the club were quite interested in it. Now, on the other hand, some of the rest of them weren't. People like Martin with his helicopter, he thought it had no place and things got a little bit heated. One of the other boys, John, he actually, I think, taught Angus how to use the drone because when Angus first came, he was horrible. He had no ability with it.'

'So what? He just came with a really spanking new drone and no ability to use it?' said Kirsten. 'Is that what he was looking for? Somebody to teach him? Otherwise, I don't see why he's there.'

'That was it. That's exactly it. He came along so somebody could teach him how to fly the drone. Week after week he's coming along. The first lot of weeks, it's ripping across the runway. He's not got a clue about the etiquette of us flying circuits, where we're putting aircraft, because we run this like an airport, or at least an airfield. We're all stowed in a safe place. The planes have certain places to go. You don't go on a runway if there're other people there with other aircraft on it. That's the thing about it— you have to take part. You have to see the whole club and the whole airfield as being alive and running. Otherwise, you end up with accidents.'

'Accidents?' said Kirsten. 'How bad an accident can you have here?'

'Well, that's the thing. You see, we had a lady member, Kathy, came along. Kathy, she'd been with us for about nine months before Angus started. She had this small plastic quite cheap, radio controlled aircraft run on battery. It wasn't much, but you've seen us out there. Excuse me, but we're not going to turn down a lady member. The thing about Kathy was she was mid-30s. Very nice without being rude about it. She was very nice, and so we were quite happy. You can imagine that some of the guys here, they don't have that many female friends. Even those of us who do, she was very pleasant. Very pleasant, very easy to get on with.'

'Very easy to look at,' said Kirsten. 'Don't worry, it's fine. It's not some sort of disgusting thing to find a woman attractive. As long as everyone behaves themselves, there's no problem, is there?'

'No, there isn't. On that side of things, everybody did behave themselves, but then Angus came along with his drone. Like I said, he doesn't understand the rules and what's going on. It must have been about the fifth or sixth week of him being there. Basically, he sent his drone across the runway as Ian was coming in to land. He clipped the wing of Ian's aircraft, which spun out of control and basically plunged straight into the face of Kathy. Hit her quite a clout too. We had to take her to the hospital and that. She was fine afterwards but had some bruising. I know it was quite a bash, but she was fine. However, that was it. She was finished with the club. As you can imagine, that made a few of the members quite annoyed.'

'What did Angus say about that?'

'Well, that was the thing. If he had simply apologised and

all that, made some sort of reparation, people wouldn't have been bothered, but it just didn't happen. He was actually more interested in whether or not his drone was okay. The other thing was that he seemed to have a timescale to learn by. He kept saying to me and to the rest of them, 'Oh, another, whatever, seven weeks, another six weeks, another eight weeks. I need to get this ready. I need to have this done.' He never said what for. I don't know if he was going for a job or what. It was very bizarre.'

Kirsten stood up with her cup of tea and looked out of the window. 'You've got a good wide space for it here though. I'd imagine flying a drone here would be quite simple. Did you ever put any obstacles up?'

'Obstacles?' said Donny. 'Not really, but now you come to mention it, Angus sort of laid out a thing. Nobody ever quite understood what he was doing, but it was like he would want to land the drone over this bit and then go move across to here, and it had to go at a certain height here. He had something in his head that he had to achieve, but we never understood. He never would tell anybody what for. Of course, that hacked everyone off because the runway was part of this and he just wandered onto it. That's why Kathy got a plane in the face. Do you know how hard it is to get a female member here? I advertise, we put the word around and say it's for everyone, but it's not, is it? You don't get that many female members wanting to fly model aircraft. We finally get one and she's a lovely person, and that happens.'

Kirsten continued to stare out the window, but dug deeper with Donny. 'Is Angus still here? He's still part of the club?'

'We haven't seen him in about six weeks. He just all of a sudden didn't come. I know he worked on the rigs so we were used to the idea that he might not pitch up for a week or two, maybe three, but he would still come after that. We maybe haven't seen him in about, as I say, five or six weeks.'

'Is there anything else you can tell me about him?'

'Just one thing. If we get really strong winds here, we cancel. You can imagine we can't fly aircraft in really strong winds, but Angus would say to me, 'I need to be here. I need to practice. I need to do this, whatever the weather.' That was the thing that got me, whatever the weather. I'd say to him, 'Why?' It was one day he was out here, hailstones, everything coming down, and I know, because I drove past. We'd cancelled because it was ridiculous. I look out and there he is trying to fly this drone in that ridiculous weather. Wasn't getting very far either. Why? Why would you bother? I never understood that. What was so important about flying this drone to him?'

'Thank you, Donny,' said Kirsten. 'Thank you for this cup of tea. I'm afraid I'm going to have to leave it now. Can you tell me, do you get many people watching your club?'

'Excuse me? Watching the club? We don't get anybody watching the club. You might occasionally get somebody drifting past, but no.'

'Anyone with binoculars, things like that?'

'No,' said Donny. 'We don't get anybody like that. Why do you ask?'

'There's a man on the far side of the football pitch. He's looking over here.'

'Well, he's probably watching them flying about, watching the aircraft.'

'No,' said Kirsten. 'He's watching here, where we are. Those binoculars haven't lifted once to follow an aircraft. They haven't turned left or right. He is watching us for some reason.

Do you have anybody in your life trying to follow you? Do you have any personal problems? Do you have any problems on the council?' Kirsten's tone had gone quite serious and flat.

'No,' said Donny. 'Nothing, nothing controversial, nothing I'm aware off. Should I be aware of something?'

'Not that I know of,' said Kirsten, 'but I am investigating something so I don't know if I'm being tailed. There's only the one door out of here, isn't there?'

'That's correct.'

'Okay,' said Kirsten, 'Can you grab me a model aircraft? One you don't mind me dropping in a hurry?'

'Look behind you,' said Donny. 'See that one? The small one. It's broke anyway. It's just parts. We pull bits off of that to go and fix other things. Stick that under your arm and you'll want to take one of those controllers over there. That one doesn't work, so take that, head on out, and as long as you don't try and pretend to fly it, it will be good cover for you.'

'Thank you, Mr Owens. Absolute pleasure speaking to you.' With that, Kirsten took her dummy controller and model aircraft out of the hut, walking back across the field to where the rest of the men were standing. She got some strange looks as she put the model on the ground and one man leaned over to say, 'That won't fly, you know,' to which Kirsten said, 'Yes, I know,' but her eyes kept flicking up to the man at the far end of the field. Now that she was closer, she could see the man was wearing a black leather jacket and a pair of glasses. He had jeans underneath, blue and some black shoes. Carefully, Kirsten put her model aircraft on the ground and then took the controller in her hand. The man had the binoculars up again and he was looking towards her. Kirsten leaned over to the man beside her, feigning to ask the question. When

73

the binoculars turned to look slightly away, she dropped her controller and ran. It took the man about three seconds before his binoculars swept back and he could see the advancing Kirsten.

Kirsten saw the man turn and start to sprint along the side of the football pitch. *No you don't*, she thought. *I'm going to have you*, and she cut left harder across the pitch round the back of the carpark. She knew the road the man was on only went one way and he'd have to cut across moor land, if he didn't follow the road itself. As she came out of the carpark, she could see he had taken that option and was already halfway across a field. The heather was thick and hard to run through, but Kirsten was light enough on her feet and she skipped, hopped, jumped and ran. She felt she was gaining ground. Although she'd worked in Lewis and especially around the Stornoway area, she wasn't familiar with this moor and where it led. This particular patch seemed to go past a very small loch and then round the side of a hill. The man was maybe one hundred metres in front of her now, but she knew she was gaining.

She watched him stumble, fall over and pick himself up, running as hard as he could. It was then she saw the road ahead and the car that was waiting. There were no lights on it, so surely there was no one inside. If she'd had time to stop, Kirsten would have admired the view either side of her, because although it was grey and windy, the moor swept a strange mixture of whites, browns, and greens with the occasional ripple of water of an odd loch rising on either side at times. The hills were covered in a similar blanket until you got higher and into more rocky terrain.

The man reached the road, which had a barbed wire fence in front of it. It took him a moment to put a foot on a fence post and get himself over. Kirsten was not far behind and she reckoned she could gain ground by simply hurdling it. As she got closer, she realized the fence was much higher than she thought and instead, jumping off her left foot, she leapt with her hands out in front of her, landing on the other side into a roll and coming up on her feet. Having regained her balance, she ran hard for the car and heard the car door slam shut. As she reached the rear of the car, the wheels turned, and it began to roll as she jumped forward putting her hands halfway down the rear of it before they slid onto the number plate and off again. She hit the ground hard, but looked up, her officer's eyes reading the number plate, committing those letters and numbers to memory.

Why were you looking at me? she thought. *Why on earth were you looking at me?* Angus wanted a drone. What did he do with it? Why do you not want me to know?

Chapter 9

Macleod stood awaiting the arrival of the platform manager and his colleague Hope. After they had interviewed the platform staff, they'd sat together sifting through numerous piles until they came up with twenty persons who were in the vicinity of the kitchen area and who had enough time to take Angus Macleod back there and to have killed him. In total, there were nineteen men and one woman, all from a range of different places. There were some from Shetland, Orkney, some from the mainland, Aberdeen way and further afield, and a number from Lewis as well. That was the thing about the oil rig, it was a community all on its own, one that brought all together from many different places. A community that no one saw, and yet Macleod needed to understand the undercurrents that had caused this terrible wave that had struck.

Macleod had given instructions that he wanted to search the rooms and belongings of all twenty of these people, but he had to give the platform manager some time to allow it. He was quite keen to have the persons there when they searched their rooms, keen to let Hope do the searching, while he gauged the faces and the reactions of the people. Sometimes you told more from that than you did from finding things within their room.

As Macleod stood awaiting the arrival of Hope, he stared at the corridors around him. He was standing in the accommodation block, but it seemed to be permanently busy. Sure, there were people asleep in rooms, others traveling back and forward on their time off, maybe heading for the gym facility, off to watch films, out to the canteen to eat. That was what was becoming more apparent to Macleod; the rig was like a city that never slept. Through the night, people were still there, working; come the day, people were working, people were eating, people were keeping fit, or doing whatever else spare time allowed. There were conversations happening in the canteen area, people talking to each other. There was more than work that went on on an oil rig platform.

Maybe some bored person who had made a deal that would talk about life offshore, life back at home. There were worries and concerns about wives, husbands, loved ones. This place was as complex as any village or town, but unlike a village or a town, Macleod saw a place that wasn't in shock. Maybe that was because of the need to perpetually keep going. Oil didn't stop; the rig didn't stop working. To shut down could cause more problems than to keep going. There was the work to focus on, the work to keep them from coming together and dealing with their shock, and that made it all the harder to read.

In a town, you'd expect some sort of memorial. You'd have the local vicar pulling people together, residents' association, worrying that this might happen again. Macleod wondered if the same fears were here. Maybe they'd surface if they had the call to muster them again. This was an uncommon occurrence,

Macleod had found out, that serious alarms were once in a while, and indeed they had to train for it, coming to muster. That was a regularity, but finding someone dead at the end of it, someone murdered, that was not normal.

Macleod felt a tap on the shoulder and turned to find his red-headed sergeant looking straight at him. 'We're good to go, Seoras,' she said. 'Mr McCallan's got it all sorted. How are you wanting to play it?'

'I suggest you do the searching. You do the looking; I'll keep an eye on the suspects.'

'That's the problem of not having the rank, isn't it?' said Hope. 'You always have to do the hard labour.'

'If my knees could take it you know I would,' said Macleod with a smile, but there was no chance of that happening. 'Besides,' he said, 'I think all these men would rather have you rifling through their stuff than me. Hope, the field's yours.'

McCallan stayed outside the first room where a middle-aged man stood looking extremely worried. This was nothing unusual for suspects to do, especially if they were innocent. Macleod gave no smile or indication that things would be okay. With the door open, Hope began her search through, occasionally holding up an item or two, but never saying much. Macleod had his notepad, occasionally writing down all the items that had been found, but in truth, he wasn't really sure what he was looking for. If anything, he was just trying to shake the box and see what would fall out. In this first room, very little by the looks of it.

The second room belonged to the only woman amongst the suspects. A woman in her mid-thirties, she seemed to be quite tough to Macleod. She had a grimace and a number of tattoos that ran up her arm. Macleod had become aware over the years that tattoos didn't always mean that someone was that rough-tough character portrayed in so many films. Indeed, a lot of genuinely goodhearted, financially astute and fair-natured people had a string of tattoos around them but in his day, it had meant something different. It was usually the rougher end of the class divide that seemed to sport them.

The woman's name was Mairi but Macleod noticed it was spelled in the Gaelic fashion. He also noticed from the information he'd been given to him by McCallan that the woman was from the Isle of Lewis. Mairi Nicholson. He looked down at the address and recognized it with just being outside Stornoway. Angus Macleod had been from Stornoway so maybe that was a connection. He made a circle with his pen but it was a very loose connection. After all, there were plenty of people here from the Isle of Lewis. For anyone who'd lived in the Islands in Scotland, rig work was always an opportunity. In places where jobs would sometimes be hard to come by, packing up and getting yourself out there was often the way of life. Three weeks off-island, three weeks at home but you could afford a house that was decent. You could keep your wife, or a husband, and the children in some sort of luxury. The search of the room finished and Hope gave a little shake of the head to Macleod.

'I've got a bad feeling we're not going to get very far, boss,' said Hope. 'Even if you brought something out with you, you're not going to leave it here. It's going to be elsewhere on the rig and that's going to be awkward to search with all the regulations. I know McCallan's told us we can go wherever we want, but that's with someone, always with someone.'

Macleod smiled at Hope. 'Come on, let's get this done and shake the box. Like you, I have had next to no sleep over the last twenty-four hours and like you, I want to get back off this floating village as soon as but we won't do that until we come up with something, so let's crack on.' It was on the tenth room that they visited, that Macleod realized he had someone else from Stornoway, DJ Macleod. Again, he was in his mid-thirties, but this time lived right in the centre of Stornoway if Macleod read the address correct. As Hope searched the man's room, Macleod took him to one side.

'Are you aware of a Mairi Nicholson on the rig, sir?' asked Macleod.

'Yes,' said, Donald John. 'I know her from home. Don't really speak to her much here. I used to speak to her a lot when we were younger.'

'How do you mean?' asked Macleod.

'We went to school and that. We used to go out in the evenings.'

'Out in the evenings? I take it you were both at the main school in Stornoway.'

'That's correct and, in the evenings, like most of us, we used to go out to the castle grounds. Drunk a few bottles with Mairi in my time. Then a bit more than that, if you don't mind me not being coarse.'

Macleod surveyed the man and he was certainly in fine shape for mid-thirties, his arms were muscular and his shoulders wide. He had an enviable crop of hair, jet black, not going grey like Macleod's.

'Have you kept in touch?' asked the inspector.

'Oh no,' said, Donald John. 'The thing is that you drift away. I have a wife and kids now. Mairi, well, she had a husband. I think she's on her own now. I'm not 100% sure, but if I pass her, I'll say, hello. That's about it though. Long time ago, we were just kids playing around, finding out about the better things in life. Close though. Good times. I enjoyed them. Happily do them again.'

Macleod frowned. There was a part of him that hated when people had a wasted life, a wasted youth, and hadn't made something of themselves. It was ridiculous— he should be happy. During his upbringing, he had been much more staid until he got married and his wife had brought him out of his shell, not too far, certainly not to break any of the conventions of the island, but maybe there was a part of him that regretted not being wilder in his youth. He'd always feared he would go off track. Lost to the demon drink or carried away by the worries of the world. That's what they preached out here. That's what they told you and yet here they were, those who had run amuck in the castle grounds; they're earning a decent living. So much for education. All he got to do was walk around and pick up the mess everyone left behind. Sometimes life was unfair. Maybe it was time he got to enjoy it a lot more.

There it was. That thing again. That nagging doubt that he should be doing this. That maybe he should be retired. He glanced at Hope, looking at what he thought of as the modern detective. She had a sassy look, something you couldn't avoid. Sometimes he engaged Hope because he liked to play her on them.

He was never frivolous with her. In fact, Macleod had come to realize in some ways, she was quite classy. Something that had taken time to dawn on him, but she was also thorough and dogged when it came to investigations. She was here on merit. Here because he had picked her, decided that she should stay in his team and he knew he didn't choose lightly. Maybe it was time to hand it all over to her. The new breed of inspectors coming through. They understood modern life better than he did but then he thought that her instinct wasn't like his, wasn't like Kirsten's. Doggedness only got you so far.

It had taken almost five hours to conduct a quick search of everyone's room and Macleod had collapsed on his bed trying to grab five minutes before he met up with Hope again but she was keen. Heard a knock on his door after barely sixty seconds.

'Oh, sorry, Seoras. I didn't realize you wanted to go for a sleep.'

'I wasn't sleeping. It's just— well, I'm not that young, am I? I mean, look at you. You're going strong. I'm not, and I don't know what time of day it is. I look at you and you're as fresh as a daisy.'

'I don't think so,' said Hope. 'I certainly don't feel it. That's why I want to get cracked through this and then maybe we can get some sleep. Here,' she said and threw down a small folder onto the desk in the room. Macleod made his way to a chair, pulled one back for Hope in a chivalrous fashion she'd begun to accept from him. Then he joined her sitting on his own seat.

'We got nothing from the search. Nothing except the fact that DJ Macleod used to be the boyfriend of Mairi Nicholson. Both from Lewis.'

'I was looking at this, sir, and if you notice, there's quite a few people from Lewis.'

'There's quite a few people from a lot of places, Hope,' said Macleod. 'That's just the way it goes out here on the rigs. We've all got to come in from somewhere. I know it feels like you're coming somewhere central, but people have to come out of towns and villages. Bound to be a number here linked to each other. I'm sure if we went outside from here, there'd be plenty people from Lewis and Stornoway as well?'

'Yes, there is sir but I thought I would do a bit of checking. I've got the laptop with me. Hang on a second. Let's start filtering through. Andrea Romain was good enough to furnish me with the movements of all the people on and off the rig. Now if I just search through by names, I should be able to have a look at something that came to mind.'

'Like what?' asked Macleod. He was always impressed with anybody that could operate a spreadsheet. He would happily go back to index cards any day of the week.

'Well,' said Hope, 'what I'm going to do is out of the twenty, I want to see if there's any pattern of when they were on the rig. As you know most people work a three-week pattern. Some have slightly different ones but they don't all arrive at once and go away at once. It's a constant coming and going, a constant flow. I want to see who's been here a lot with Angus Macleod— look at the possible contact between them.'

'Knock yourself out,' said Macleod. 'Don't try and explain how you do it. Just tell me the answer when you get it.'

He saw Hope smile. She reached down behind her, pulling out the hair tie, letting her red hair flop around. It was one of those innocuous sights that would please any man but rather than make him focus on Hope, it actually made Macleod think about Jane, his partner back at his house. He really needed to phone her; he hadn't since he came on the rig. It was true that she didn't expect anything from him, especially at the start of a case because he was always involved, so deep in that he forgot about the outside world, but she deserved better than that. He made a note in his book clearly at the front, large block letters, Jane, and a circle around it.

'That's interesting,' said Hope.

'What is it?'

'Slide over, Seoras. Look at the screen.' Macleod did so and was soon shaking his head. 'Don't show me graphs and charts and different things. Just tell me what it means.'

'Well, you see what I've done is I've filtered out the names of the twenty people tied them in and got a percentage of time when they were here with Angus Macleod. Now there's five of them registering in the top 90% so they were on the rig 90% of the time Angus Macleod was on the rig. In fact, now that I look at it their coming and going dates are not that far different and they seem to have been that way for over a year.'

'Okay,' said Macleod, 'what about it?'

'Look at the names,' said Hope. 'We've got a Macleod, a Macleod, another Macleod, Mairi Nicholson, and a John Nicholson.'

Macleod looked at Hope. 'You're telling me these five people have been here basically, all the time that Angus Macleod has?'

'It's exactly what I'm telling you, Seoras, but more than that, look at the addresses. Four out of the five Stornoway, the Isle of Lewis; they are from where our boy's from. If you look at the ages, they're all within seven years of each other.'

'Seven years in Stornoway, if that's where they were brought up,' said Macleod, 'a high possibility they knew each other through school. On the islands, quite often they go through very small primary schools, and on Lewis, there's one big secondary; it's why everybody knows everyone. It's one of the joys and the woes of it,' said Macleod. Suddenly the tiredness was gone. The fatigue was fading away. Jane would have to wait.

Chapter 10

Ross had taken the phone call from Macleod late in the evening. The inspector wanted some groundwork done on five names from the oil platform; three Macleod, two Nicholson. Four of them on the Isle of Lewis, one in the Cairngorms on the mainland. It'd probably be too much to start out that night. The least he could do was get hold of Kirsten, give her a heads-up about where she was looking next. Ross made a call to Stewart and found that she was in a hotel room, recovering from quite a physical chase.

'I'm a bit scuffed, Ross, to be honest, but there's nothing that won't heal. I did get the number plate and ran it through. It seems the guy hired a car, so I went down to the car hire place but it's all false. False name, false address. I checked with the Fort William police. They went back to the house for me but the couple there knew nothing about this man. He's obviously here for a reason but I'm not sure what. Is he covering something up, or is he seeking information like us? Is he watching me to find out what I find?'

'You're like the boss,' said Ross. 'Coming at things from strange angles. Most people would put that guy down as a culprit covering up. Not you. You see things in different ways.

How's your brother, by the way?'

'He's where he needs to be,' said Kirsten, 'but he's not great. The doctors still really don't know what's up with him. All I know is he's got a lot worse than he used to be and he needs twenty-four-hour care. Something I can't give him.'

Ross could hear the pain in her voice. Rather than butt in with some comment, he let the silence hang, letting Kirsten know that he was with her but in the quiet, not in some offhanded way. 'I've got an address for you. Donald John Macleod. You have to go to the main school in Stornoway. See what you can find out about him. See what the Stornoway police know. You probably don't need to do anything until the morning, so get yourself some rest. I need to get out to the Cairngorms. Got a house to check out there.

'There's three other houses for you to chase up as well in Lewis. There's a Mairi Nicholson, an Ian Macleod, and a James Macleod. The boss thinks they might all be tied in together and therefore, there might be something underneath. He hasn't got anything on them. There's no physical evidence. There's nothing to tie them in the rig except for the fact that they're there all the time with each other. He says it's a spade job, dig and dig as hard as you can. Neighbours everything, whatever you can get hold of, and then feed it back to the brainbox.' Ross heard a laugh from Stewart.

'You didn't say that in front of him?'

'No. I certainly didn't,' said Ross, 'but he is. He's the brainbox, isn't he? Even you. I should really be over there with the spade, I guess. I'm going to dig on this side. Hope will be doing the digging for him on the rig. That's what he is, the brainbox over the three spade carriers.' He heard Stewart laugh again. He needed to pick her up because he could tell the situation with her brother was definitely bringing her down.

'Okay, Ross. I'm going to get to bed soon, because frankly, I'm exhausted. I'll get up early in the morning and start on the rest of it. Don't get to bed late tonight either. You got plenty to look up.'

'Don't worry about me,' said Ross. 'You know, always in bed by ten.'

With that, he looked up at the clock and thought, *There's no way in hell I'll be in bed by ten*. Ross looked up contact numbers for the main school, and spent the next hour trying to get hold of someone who could talk to him about records. He got the usual thing of *could it wait until the morning*, and he decided it couldn't, because by 6:00 a.m., his boss will be asking him what he'd found out. If he said, 'I haven't gone anywhere, and neither have I found anything online,' he knew he would hear Macleod grump.

That was the thing about him. The inspector liked to be full-on with cases. He had a thing that said, 'Leads run cold. The more distance you put between the crime, and the time of solving it, the less likely you are to get it right. Do it while it's hot. Do it while it's there. Especially because they'll think you're getting close early, and then they panic . . . and then they make mistakes.'

Ross had learned a lot from him, but he also saw that Macleod was changing over these last few months— beginning to doubt whether he was the one for the job. Ross had never heard anything more ridiculous and actually thought it was more about him being weary. Macleod seemed to be tiring of what he was doing. It was quite a surprise, especially since he had his partner Jane around. She certainly had changed him from when Ross had first met him back on the case in the

Black Isle. She had calmed the man, taken away a frustration that he seemed to have about him.

Ross had his own partner but he wasn't there tonight, off at some conference. That was another reason to stay late and get things done. He'd be going home to an empty bed, going home to an empty flat. Ross liked people and he liked having someone with him in life.

When Ross finally got hold of someone who could handle the records of the main school, he had to wait half an hour while they drove into the building to access the records properly. Mairi Nicholson had been in the same year as DJ Macleod. Ian and James were also in that year. Alastair Nicholson was Mairi's brother. He was five years younger, as was Angus, the deceased.

'Is there anyone in particular who would know about these people?' asked Ross. 'Any teachers? Anyone who I would be able to speak to about them?'

There was a little cough on the end of the line. The woman who was helping him with his inquiries seemed a little put out.

'I'm not asking for anything special,' said Ross. 'Is there somebody to give me an overview about how they were?'

'I really shouldn't say this, but—'

Oh yes, thought Ross, *that's always the bit that you really should say if you put that in front of it.*

The woman continued, 'There was a teacher here— Alan, Alan Carmichael. He's not with us anymore; in fact, he's not teaching, but I do have an address for him, or at least I have the address that he used to be at. He would know quite well about Mairi and certainly in connection with the rest of the boys. They were quite tight from what I understand.'

'As a teacher, he was tight with Mairi?' queried Ross.

'No,' she said. 'He wasn't tight with Mairi; he was sleeping with her. She was just about eighteen at the time but even so, it was all kept quite quiet. Nothing proved, but it was dealt with. His wife found out though but I know he was a daft one. He was found up at Castle Grounds with them at one point so he might know stuff, but like I said I don't really want to bring any of that up again.'

'Don't worry,' said Ross. 'I'll be very discreet and you absolutely were correct in bringing it up. If you can pass me the number I'll get on to him tonight.' Ross looked up at the clock. It was already eleven. Making a note of the number, Ross then proceeded to ring it and a woman answered the phone.

'Hello, my name's DC Ross from the Inverness Police Station. I'm trying to get hold of a Mr Carmichael.'

There was a swear down the phone and Ross realized he'd hit a very large nerve.

'Well, I hope you want to book him and sling him into a cell.'

'I'm sorry?'

'I said I hope you're trying to book him and sling him in a cell. I washed my hands of that dirty pervert, washed my hands of it. Do you hear? It's over fifteen years ago.'

'I'm sorry, who am I speaking to?' asked Ross.

'Jenny, Jenny Brockley. The Mr Carmichael you're looking for used to be my husband. I was Jenny Carmichael. I'm now Jenny Brockley, single and keeping it that way.'

'Right,' said Ross, realizing that he'd have to be careful and not tread on any eggshells. 'I hope you don't mind me asking, but I would really appreciate being taken through what happened. I'm sorry if it brings back bad memories but at the moment I need to gain some information on Mr Carmichael, and also a contact if you've got one.'

'The story's quite easy,' said Jenny. 'The story is he shagged a girl at that school, left me in disgrace. Everyone knew it. Everyone knew about it, except me. I knew nothing. She used to walk past me, she'd walk past our house, skirt so high you'd wonder you couldn't see her knickers. She was something else. We left the island pretty sharp once it sort-of-half came out.

'School kept it quiet, but of course, he wasn't going to get a job again, on the grapevine and that. I ended up being the only one bringing any money in, so I told him to sling his hook. I'd given him fifteen years of my life at that point and I was something, do you know that? I was better than what she was, better looking than she was, a better person than she was. I just wasn't the manipulating bitch that she was. That's your story, officer. That's it in a nutshell. Would you mind if I go to bed?'

'I'm sorry to have bothered you, but it's quite essential I get hold of him. Would you have any sort of contact for him?' The woman sounded like she was about to cry. When she came back, she sniffed out a number. 'Thank you for that,' said Ross. 'I'm sorry to have brought this up but the nature of what I'm investigating means that I have to. Please take care and thank you for your assistance.' There was more crying on the phone. Ross asked twice if she was okay, but then the phone went down.

That was the thing about this job. Just when you thought you were on the go, you were getting somewhere, something came in and blindsided you. Ross stood up and walked to the canteen inside the station, sitting down with a black coffee and looking at the far wall, where a poster told him how to eat healthily, quoting five types of fruit for each day. Maybe this is what was getting to Macleod. It got to Ross, but he hadn't been in this game as long. Maybe picking apart people's woes and hurts just became too much.

As he drunk the last dregs of his coffee, he looked across and saw that it was close to midnight. Maybe he could ring in the morning, try and track Carmichael then. Or maybe he would do it tonight. The man was in bed, but who cared. He deserved it. Ross made his way back to the office, picked up the phone, and dialled the number he'd been given by Jenny Brockley. It rang several times and Ross was expecting an answering machine to kick in, but none came and the phone kept on ringing. Just as Ross was about to put the receiver back down, he heard a voice from the other end.

'Hello? Hello?' It was a woman's voice and clearly, she had been asleep.

'I'm sorry to disturb you, ma'am, this is the DC Ross from Inverness Police Station. To who am I speaking, please?'

'Layla, my name is Layla. Layla George.'

'I am sorry to disturb you, Layla,' said Ross, 'but I'm looking for Mr Carmichael on this number.'

'Well, I'm looking for him too,' said the woman. 'He disappeared. About seven or eight weeks ago.'

'Disappeared?' queried Ross. 'In what way did he disappear?'

'I came home and he had packed up the bag. Said he had a bit of work up north and then he went.'

'When you say up north, where do you live?'

'Newquay, Cornwall,' said the woman.

'Do you know how far up north?'

'No,' said the woman. 'I don't. All I know is he said he had a bit of work. It came his way from somebody he used to know.'

'Did he give that person a name?' asked Ross.

'No,' said the woman. 'He didn't. I asked him more about it but he didn't say anything. Very tight-lipped. Which was unlike him.'

'How long have you been together?' asked Ross.

'Well, we've been seeing each other for about six months, but we've really only got the relationship together the last three. I just guessed he'd had enough and he was off. He certainly didn't come back. I thought that was unusual, though because he's left some items in the house.'

'What do you mean by items?'

'He's left his guitars for a start. He likes his guitars. I'm not sure why he would leave them.'

'Did you file him as a missing person at all?'

The woman laughed. 'Hey, he was just a casual boyfriend. We might have slept together and that, but we weren't bonded. If he took off because he finds somebody better he has had enough, well, there you go. Surely he'll come for his stuff at some point. I was sure he'd send the address through.'

'You've said it's been what, six to eight weeks? Nearly two months,' said Ross. 'Maybe worth a phone call all that?'

'Oh, I did ring him. Nothing coming back. You get an answer machine. Nothing else.'

'Okay, Layla, I tell you what. I want you to go and make yourself a large coffee, or whatever it is that you drink. There's going to be a police officer coming around to your house. He's going to want to take a statement and some details. He might want to search the place as well. I'm afraid we're looking for Mr Carmichael quite earnestly at the moment and I think he might be able to help us.'

'I do have work in the morning,' she said.

'Well, if need be, we can ring your boss and explain. I'm

afraid we need to make some further inquiries tonight. Give me your address and as I say, feel free to get changed if you've been in bed or whatever but there'll be an officer round shortly.'

Ross hung up the phone. It was now half-past midnight and he would need to call the station down in Newquay and run through with them the questions he needed to be asked and everything else to go along with it. 'Well,' he thought. 'I hope you're getting a good night's sleep, Kirsten, because I'm not.'

Chapter 11

Hope had been ready for her shower. Having searched all those lockers inside in the place that had such stuffy air, she'd built up quite a sweat. The last thing she wanted to do was to lie down in bed feeling mucky. She was also feeling like her back was about to collapse. She had bent down going through cupboard after cupboard. The rooms were compactly designed, so underneath all the bunks were cupboards where the workers could store their gear. There was a wardrobe as well, but she constantly found herself on her knees, and they were sore as well. Or maybe it was just the tiredness, she'd been up on her feet for over twenty-four hours, catching the odd nap here and there for five minutes. That night, Macleod had said they needed to grab four to six hours sleep, and she was ready for it.

The showers were remarkably good. Hope felt a little refreshed, if somewhat sleepy. She made her way back to the bed. Normally at home, she would sleep with nothing on, but the chances of getting disturbed here meant that she'd put on her pyjamas. She certainly wasn't going to stand up, fling on a flimsy dressing gown, and answer the door here. Who knew who would come? Certainly not John Allen.

The name rang in her head. She hadn't rung John. She'd been so busy, so exhausted. Maybe she should ring him now, and then Hope noticed the clock, 1:00 in the morning. Maybe not. I should do it tomorrow or later today. Yes, that was it. Later today, wasn't it? It was today. Well, yes, it was always today, but there was last night, and there was this morning, and then there was today. Yes, time was just running on and on and getting ahead of her.

Seoras was quite the taskmaster. Part of her wondered if he was even going to sleep. Things would be taking over in his head. He had called Ross with the information for the constable back at base. Ross would have to sift through everything. They'd have their investigating to do and that would make Macleod jumpy. He was always happier when he was doing the investigating himself, happier when he was there in charge. When people were off on their own, he got anxious.

It had taken Hope a while to realize just how privileged she was that he would send her off, usually, away from him to handle another line of investigation. It had taken a long time to realize the trust that was involved. Now, they were stretched because Stewart was out on Lewis. That normally would have been Hope's thing if it hadn't had been for Stewart's brother not being that well. Good old Ross back at base picking through the bones. Hope smiled as she curled up in bed. There was only one thing missing— John Allen curling up behind her, rubbing his hand across her neck like he had last time, and then rubbing his hand over places. And then he was just lying there with her.

She'd enjoyed that. feeling his breath on her neck, but just holding her gently, not looking for anything else until he had started to snore. It was hardly romantic but Hope had had enough of romance, had enough of men wooing her in their way. She just wanted somebody to be with, somebody normal, somebody who wouldn't try and control her. What was it? If you had any sort of looks about you, there were men that just wanted to own you. She shook her head into a pillow, closing her eyes, trying to get to sleep. It wasn't easy with the noise outside on the rig, and people still going by on their business. Hope was used to a quieter place, but soon her eyes became heavy, and she started to drift off.

Hope was unsure of the time when she began to wake, but something in her said it was maybe an hour, maybe slightly longer. She went to yawn and to stretch her arms, but something told her not to. There was a faint sound. Then she heard a footstep. Tensing up, she listened intently. When she could hear the faint breathing, it was only a few feet away at the desk. Slowly, Hope opened her eyes and tried to focus in the dark of the room. She could see very little, but slowly, a shape appeared at the desk.

Hope was six-foot tall, and certainly was not afraid to engage any man, but the one before her was broad-shouldered and much taller than she. She saw legs that were like the proverbial tree trunks, and she wondered how she would take him down, if he proved to be violent. Clearly, he was here for some reason and not for her, for she'd been asleep, and he hadn't done anything towards her. Instead, he was beginning to shuffle through papers on the desk.

A small torchlight came on. She was aware that he was mumbling slightly, possibly reading something to himself. It was her case notes on the table, and the man started to flick through her little pocketbook, and then moved across to some other papers. Hope was gently pulling back her covers, ready to swing her legs around. She didn't want to move too quickly, in case the bunk creaked and give away her position. Instead, she drew them back carefully before swinging her legs quite slowly and moving on to her backside. She stood up behind the man. She saw he was studying printed notes, a suspect list. Hope moved up behind him and then quickly swung her arm round while grabbing his left arm with her other hand. She drove his wrist up behind his back, then went to kick hard into the back of his legs to drive him to the floor, but the man didn't budge. She felt the arm pushing back against her, freeing itself. Then there was an elbow right to her face, sending Hope backwards. She smacked her head on the top of the bunk above before falling to the floor.

Desperately, she tried to scramble to her feet, ready for another onslaught. She managed to throw both hands up as a foot came towards her. Her hands took most of the blow, but she still fell back onto the floor. Thankfully, the man then made a run for it. Hope cried out loudly, as she tried to scramble back to her feet. As the door opened, she realized the man had a hood on, something covering his face, and he ran quickly down the corridor. As she made it to the hall, she saw the man shove someone over hard and turn down another corridor. Hope followed, recognizing the man on the floor was her boss. There were coffee stains up the wall, and Macleod was groaning. He tried to sit back up. 'What on earth?'

'A man was in my room,' said Hope, and ran past Macleod straight down the corridor the culprit had taken. The corridor ended in a door that led out to the side of the rig. As Hope opened it, she felt someone grab her by the throat. She kicked hard, but nothing would stop the pair of hands that pushed her onto the railing of the gangway that ran along the outside of the accommodation block. She felt her legs begin to lift, and realized the man was going to tip her right over and she'd fall far below. Normally, you wouldn't be able to tip over the top of this gangway, but the man had lifted her so that her shoulders had gone over it and her legs were now scrambling, looking for any perches.

As she failed to control them, she realized her best hope might actually be to let him send her over the top and hang on the outside. Tipping her head back, she flung her hands out, managed to grab on to the guard mesh that ran alongside as her legs sailed over the top of her head. Desperately, she clung on with her hands and her body was flung into the guard mesh. Because she was in bare feet, she was able to cling with her toes as well. As the man shook the guard mesh, Hope hung on for grim life, hearing the sea down below her. The oil rig as usual, was lit up so she could easily see the handholds, but the man had a snood across his face, preventing her from identifying him.

'McGrath, McGrath, are you okay?' With the sound of Macleod's voice, Hope's attacker ran off along the gangway, and she started to scramble back up and over. By the time, she made her way back onto the gangway, Macleod opened the door, but she didn't wait for him. Instead, she ran hard, following where her culprit would have been. She managed to see his foot disappear up a ladder, heading for the top of the accommodation block. It was now that the rain began. A heavy shower with hail mixed in it, battering down. As she climbed the ladder, her feet were cold and her pyjamas became sodden quickly. As she reached the top of the accommodation block, she had an icy feeling running through her.

Hope saw no one on the top of the block. She ran along it, the size of a couple of football pitches, looking down at the edges to see if anyone had descended. There were some gangways he could drop on to, but no one was there. It took her time to run here and there, and she heard a voice shouting up at her, 'McGrath, where the heck are you? What are you doing? Are you okay, McGrath? Are you all right?'

She felt best if Seoras didn't climb the ladder, didn't come up here as he wasn't that steady on his feet, and so she made her way back towards where she had climbed up. Looking down, she saw her boss soaked through, standing in his shirt and trousers. He must have felt cold, because she was freezing. It was then she stopped and looked over the side. Below, you could see the waves crashing against the superstructure. She could hear the sea swelling. They might have picked her up; they might have been ready to drop her into the sea. It was only her quick thinking that had prevented it. If he had been in with Seoras, there's no way Macleod could have stopped him. A chill ran through her, a chill that was not coming from the wind, or the rain, or the hail. Somebody had been prepared to kill a police officer. This wasn't a normal murder. This was somebody with a lot at stake. *Where could he go?* thought Hope. *We have him, she thought. We have them.*

Chapter 12

Ross was exhausted. What had looked like a late night had turned into morning. When he received a call from Macleod, advising of Hope's escapades, he was struggling to take it all in. As for his own investigations, the Newquay police had called around to speak to Lyla George, and she had been most helpful.

Lyla and Carmichael had enjoyed a blossoming relationship, and the fact that Carmichael had disappeared was a surprise, but she had been able to pass on details of his phone and a recent photograph of him, which Ross now had in his possession. They tried to trace the phone, and the last contact had disappeared several weeks ago, but was giving a position up in the Cairngorms. He checked the OS map. Ross had seen that there were several buildings around that position.

Having checked in with the boss, Ross had decided to make his way out that morning. It was barely six o'clock when Ross was being driven into the Cairngorms area, along with uniformed officers to conduct a cursory search around where the mobile signal had last come from. Ross had also noted that the signal had been lost only a few miles from the home of Alastair Nicholson, one of the five suspects his boss was investigating. Ross would make his way over there once he checked out where the mobile signal had gone. The day was one of those spring mornings that the highlands was famous for. When the sun was out, it was glorious. Cold, but glorious. Yet in the distance, Ross could see the clouds, the ones that would bring hail, possibly snow.

It was not unusual to get snow in April up here in the mountains or even dropping down into Inverness itself. Ross always thought spring is one of the funniest seasons in the area as it could bring anything, absolutely any type of weather to you. You could get a week of glorious sunshine, temperatures shooting way up, followed the next week by snow plummeting down, back to the days of having to wear your gloves and hat. Today was starting off glorious. He would have to wait and see how it turned out.

The small cavalcade of cars arrived at a car park attached to a wood. It was one of the numerous small car parks that existed in the Cairngorms, places where people would abandon their cars to walk. The buildings the mobile phone had been in were less than half a mile away, but the roughness of the tracks that led towards them meant that driving was awkward. There were ruts in the path, which was barely wide enough for a vehicle as it was. Despite this, Ross trusted his uniformed officers and let them drive to the destination where found what appeared to be a large shed. A corrugated door some eight feet across was then slid back to reveal an empty barn. There was little inside, and Ross wondered exactly what it was doing here. Maybe it was used for storage at one point, because the building was possibly over twenty or thirty years old.

From there, they spread out until Ross came to the next

building, a small cottage. Approaching the front door, which was lilac in colour, he knocked loud enough to wake the dead, but no one answered. There were net curtains and peering inside, he saw no one. Given he was concerned for the safety of a man, Ross was prepared to break the door down, but found it to be open. Calling inside, he shouted "Police". The hallway inside led to a small lounge, which contained a TV and a number of holiday brochures. At one corner, there was a stand that contained leaflets for most of the attractions surrounding the area. Ross thought he was looking at a holiday cottage, albeit, one that wasn't maintained very well. After touring the bedrooms and the kitchen, he found no food, yet a full array of crockery, and beds that had not been slept in. They were stripped back to the bare mattress, which had also been covered with plastic sheeting. *Out of season cottage*, he thought, *or at least out of use.*

One of the officers shouted for Ross, and he made his way around to the back of the house, where along the path, he saw a small caravan. It was large enough for two people at best. One with a small kitchen area and a bed that probably had to be converted from a sofa. He walked up to the net curtains, staring inside. There was indeed a sofa that straddled either side with a gap in the middle where the floor was indistinct. Making his way to the caravan door, he found it to be unlocked. Opening it, Ross stared inside. He was in the kitchen area. It seemed neat and tidy, but when he looked to his left, he could see something on the floor. Beside him on one of the kitchen shelves, he saw a mobile phone, and wondered if that was the one they were looking for. As he got closer to the end of the caravan, he saw that on the floor were many plastic sheets, with something under them. Gingerly, he pulled them back and then discovered a foot. He called in another officer, and together, they lifted the sheets gently up, before Ross recoiled, recognizing the smell of death. Lying on the floor before him was Carmichael.

Gingerly, the pair set the plastic covering down again and stepped out of the caravan to breathe the fresh air. Ross sucked it down in lungfulls before picking up his phone. The mobile signal was faint, but he managed to place a call to the station, asking for a forensic team to come out. After that, he placed a call to Macleod, who mumbled at him, but then listened for the next five minutes. As Ross went through what he had found, his boss who had been asleep at the start of the call, was now giving his full attention. It took until about nine o'clock for the forensic team to arrive and set up, and Ross was happy to leave them to the work while he checked out the house of Alastair Nicholson.

It was only a few miles away but rather than take a uniformed officer with him, Ross simply borrowed one of the cars. Inside, he was feeling a little bit off. It was what bodies did to him. He had never got used to it, although he'd learned to control the first urges he'd had when he'd been a junior officer. He remembered seeing the first dead body of his career. A drunk had simply been left out too long in the cold, but the smell that had come with it had caused Ross to bend over and simply vomit on the ground. An inauspicious start to his days of investigating death.

Anyway, he was glad to let the forensic team do what they did, and they would soon come back to him with all the answers the scene had given them. As he drove up the winding driveway to the house that was located behind several large bushes, Ross was feeling more balanced than he had several hours ago. The house before him was a large two-story affair. Something that Ross's constable salary certainly couldn't afford. He also wondered if it were something an oil rig worker could afford as well. He realized he'd have to check out if Mr Nicholson was married. If he was, by the looks of it, it was to a banker.

Ross walked up to the front door, knocking it loudly but got no reply. He was able to see in through the front door to the hallway and noticed the large alarm keypad on the side. That would be a problem. He certainly could not simply pile in. Instead, Ross decided to take a wander around the property, and managed to find several windows he could peer through. He took out a small pair of binoculars, and with them, was able to scan each room. He started through the blinds at the front, and noted the number of what he thought must be expensive paintings on the wall. He was no expert when it came to that type of thing, but he thought he recognized the odd name on the bottom. There was certainly some expensive whiskey in a cabinet on the far side and the sofa was certainly not from the budget superstore down the road.

Ross then continued further round and found a dining room with a large amount of crystal. Again, everything spoke of class and money. The kitchen was an extensive affair once again and looked immaculate, but it was when he got round to the rear of the house, and he was able to look properly into the study that his interest was piqued. Ross noticed there were several items left on the study table.

With his binoculars, he was able to pick them out as art magazines from auction houses, brochures giving details of a sale. When he moved to the window along from this, he found a net curtain across it, and looking in was rather difficult. He had a thought and retrieved his digital camera. With that, he was able to alter the focus, able to pick up several large chunky, if blurred, images, and began to take photographs of what was inside. His interest was especially piqued by several photographs of a house. He would have to take care and get them back to forensic to try and enhance them, but something in him wondered why you would cover this window up when the study window was wide open. *Why the net curtain you struggled to see through?*

After a further cursory inspection around the ground floor, Ross made his way out to a small shed at the rear of the property. When he opened it up, he noted a number of items, including several tools. Since it was open, Ross made his way inside, and began to check the tools to see if any have been used recently, and also take photographs of them so that they would be on record, in case the body in the caravan had died at the hand of a weapon. That was a long shot and not something that he thought likely, but as he was here and the door was open, there was no harm in taking those photographs. Whether or not he could use them in evidence would be another matter, but his boss had always said, once you knew who it was, it was easier to build up the body of evidence. When you are still trying to work out who had done it, evidence always seemed harder to come by.

Ross put the camera up to his eye and focused on the point of a large chisel. It was then he heard the door shut behind him. He turned and realized that a small barrel had been tipped over as well. A liquid was pouring out of it across the floor, and Ross made for the door. As he went to open it, he found it released, but as he fell forward, somebody kicked him hard in the stomach, causing him to tumble back inside. As he looked up in horror, he saw a lighter, and a yellow flame sparked into life. The lighter was dropped, and right before him, flames leapt up, causing him to throw hands across his face and try to roll as hard as he could to the back of the shed.

The front half was ablaze, right across the doorway, preventing any chance of escape, Ross looked around him as the small shed began to fill with smoke. Behind him was a wooden wall. In front of him, another one. At his feet, he kicked hard to find the rear side of the shed was as solid as the other two that adjoined it. Smoke began to choke him. Ross made sure he knelt at the floor, keeping his head as low as he could. He began to cry out for help, but he knew his officers were nowhere near here. He was at least a mile or two away from them. He would have to do something and fast; otherwise, he would burn to death in this shed.

Chapter 13

Macleod was not happy. After being out in the rain from chasing down McGrath's intruder, he was now standing in the room that had been set aside as Jona Nakamura's temporary mortuary. The pair had searched in vain. Having raised the platform manager, Macleod along with McCallan and Hope had performed a roll call. With work in progress on the platform, it had taken a while to get the exact numbers. He had received many a stare from workers who had been woken rudely in their slumber. Having been kept from his bed, Macleod had no time for this. Any disgruntled voices were soon snapped closed.

There had been nowhere for the man to run, nowhere to hide. Macleod knew that he must be on the vessel somewhere. About two hours later, when all had been accounted for except for one person, Macleod was not surprised to find the name of the man amongst the five Stornoway suspects they narrowed down. Alastair Nicholson was the one suspect who currently didn't have a Stornoway address. Macleod sent out search parties to look for him on the rig. The howling wind and rain didn't help and the occasional smattering of hail that came across the rig left the inspector cold. When he eventually returned to his bed at around 5:00 a.m., all he wanted to do was to get a good night's sleep. However, he knew he had to check-in with Ross at six and so decided not to do any more than simply doze off in a chair.

Taking the call from Ross, he was interested to learn of the relationship between Mairi Nicholson and the school teacher. Maybe this would shed some light on what was really happening, why the murders were taking place. He also left Ross to examine Alastair Nicholson's house when he could. He knew his constable was more than able, and the rest of the houses would be covered by Stewart that day. It was after Macleod had settled back in his chair, sipping on a freshly poured cup of coffee, that the door was rapped. Thunder was probably more of an appropriate expression for it nearly came off its hinges. While opening it, he saw McCallan, the platform manager, and he was not in a good way.

'There's been a body. There's a body in the water.'

'Where?' asked Macleod.

'It was spotted about three miles off in the sea by the guard vessel. The guard vessel saw it. It's going to pick him up. I think it's a body. There's no movement. You don't get many people out there.'

'Did he have a life jacket on?' asked Macleod.

'I don't think so,' said the platform manager. 'If they don't, you won't always find them. I mean, you go down and maybe reappear on the surface sometimes, somewhere, but I don't know. I don't know about his buoyancy and what he had on. I don't know.'

Macleod could see the man was shaking. No wonder, this would be the second death on his platform in a space of a week. It was hard enough when there had been the first death, but who was to say this wasn't a murder the second time, and who was it? Yes, Alastair Nicholson was missing, but it didn't mean it that was Alastair Nicholson in the water.

Maybe Alastair knew somebody else who knew something on the platform. Macleod sighed. He didn't know what was on the platform. So far, they were still working in the dark. They'd narrowed down the suspects, had a potential idea that it could be the Stornoway crowd, but that was it. They had no idea what they'd done, who had done what to whom, or why they were doing it. So often, that was the case. Sometimes the means of deduction led you to the person, and yet the story was still hiding.

Macleod went with McCallan to the control room at the platform, and from there, they spoke to the guard vessel.

'We'll see if we can pull him in, but the water's wild here. I don't think he's alive. I'm loathe to risk any people for someone that isn't alive,' the captain of the vessel had said. 'You can understand me. . . can't you, inspector?'

Macleod had understood fully, but insisted that the man do everything possible that was safe to recover the body. Another few hours had been spent drinking coffee in the control room, listening to what was going on while Hope and Macleod pulled together the other four of the Stornoway suspects and tried to work out where they had been. Unfortunately, they'd all been alone, either working in a part of the platform or had been in their beds.

The other problem Macleod was going to have was the state the body would be in? Could Jona discover anything from it?

The guard vessel had called in that they'd managed to recover the body, and Macleod had brought Jona to the control room to issue instructions about what she wanted done with it, how to keep the body while they brought it back to the platform. When it was lifted up from the guard vessel onto the platform, Jona took the body straight away to her temporary mortuary to lie with the corpse of Angus Macleod. The inspector had joined her along with Hope for some initial viewings, and one thing Jona noted was how bashed in the face of the dead man was.

'Looks to me like somebody took a bar to the face several times, quick, rapid. I mean, look at the size of him, Inspector. You'd have to be quick with a guy like this. Hope tells me he had her by the throat and was trying to throw her over. Now, don't get me wrong, most men are physically stronger, but Hope is, by no means, a weak woman and yet he picked her up. More than that, held her like she was nothing. This is a strong man. You'd have to catch him by surprise and then attack him quickly. It looks like that's what they did, straight to the face, straight to the eyes. What I can tell you, Inspector, is that your attacker is shrewd.'

'Possibly,' said Hope. 'Maybe known to our dead victim. Maybe that's why they were able to put a bar in his face before he could react. He wasn't expecting it.'

'Maybe a fallout,' said Macleod. 'Maybe because he'd gone after you and made such a hash of it. Maybe he shouldn't have gone after you at all.'

'I'm glad you think so,' said Hope.

Macleod gave a wry smile. 'If they're starting to disagree though, it might bring the things to the surface. We still don't know what they're disagreeing on. Jona, get to it and give us your report when you're ready. We'll be outside while I try and think through what we're going to do.'

With that, Macleod had indeed stepped outside. Hope

had expected him to walk to the canteen with her, but he shook his head and he simply stood outside the room. At the canteen, people might bother him, people might come and ask questions, people might even sit down beside him. Here, stood outside what was in effect a mortuary, people would know he was busy, and yet Macleod wasn't. He was merely leaning up against the wall, thinking through what was happening. Leaning up against the wall was better. It was harder to fall asleep. Sitting down in the canteen, his face could end up in a bowl of Krispies for all he knew.

Half an hour later when he hadn't come to the canteen, Hope had returned, holding a sandwich and a cup of coffee. 'You could just go to your own room if you want, if you're trying to stay away from people,' said Hope. Macleod grunted. Hope continued, 'Just spoke to Ross as well. Turns out that he has found a dead body. Forensics are on to it, and they reckon it's Carmichael, the school teacher. I think that's worth a chat to Mairi Nicholson.'

'Absolutely,' said Macleod. 'You take that. Find out her side of the story, and find out which of the other five were part of it as well, if they were all there at the time. Who knows what they were up to?' Hope nodded and made her way to find Mairi Nicholson. Macleod was left alone again with his thoughts. *Did it have something to do with the school teacher? Did they know all the man had been doing at the school?*

Mairi Nicholson had been seventeen from what Ross had said previously, so the man wasn't performing a sexual offense. He was, however, abusing his position and clearly his marriage as well. What would that have to do with anything on the oil rig? Who killed him? Macleod would need to know when the man died. If it was several weeks ago, it could be anyone from the oil rig that had been back on the mainland or back on the island. One way or another, he'd have to track down their movements. It was getting to a point where he needed to re-interview them. Now he had more questions to ask.

It had gone from a simple coming onto an oil rig, a one-off, maybe a chance encounter for things that have gone wrong in the past, to suddenly becoming heavily involved in a murder case. There were three bodies, two killed out here, one killed back in the mainland, and a group of people who all knew each other. Macleod would need to interview the suspects again, but he wanted to know exactly who this was. It was allegedly Alastair Nicholson, but he needed it proven. The door to the makeshift mortuary opened while Macleod was leaning against it, so he nearly fell through the door. He was caught by Alan Corran, Jona Nakamura's assistant. He invited the inspector in. Jona was washing her hands, and she turned to the inspector with a smile on her face.

'Well, I can definitely identify him for you. It is Alastair Nicholson. In his medical record, it talks about him having a small operation on the calf of his leg, football injury or something. The scar is right there. Everything else about matches as well. His medical shows his size, his hair colour, and from the photograph we've got sent through from the records, I'd say it's him, well-bashed up to the point where his face is almost unrecognizable. This was pretty brutal. They wanted to make sure he was dead, really make sure he was dead.'

'It makes sense, Jona,' said Macleod. 'Look at the size of the man. Like we said before, look what he did to Hope. If you're going to toss somebody like this in the water, you're either going to trip him up, or he's going to be immobile when you shove him off a platform. I think there's places around here where you could simply drop him out, barriers you could move out of the way, or you could then push the body through. The hard bit would be getting to one of these quiet spots in the first place, unless he thought he was coming for a rendezvous, unless Nicholson thought or panicked and tried to get someone to meet him. The guys on the rig, they'll understand the meeting places, they'll understand where you can get away. Once they've shoved him off into the water, then he's gone. That's about the best they can hope for, no body, no statements, nothing, just a man who went and attacked a police officer. Who knows who's with him? They're probably expecting Nicholson's body never to come back up. By the time it does wash ashore somewhere, it's been so tainted by the sea, there's nothing more to learn. It's time to haul these four back in, work at what's been going. It's time to make the connections.'

'I guess you need to inform the next of kin as well.'

'That's my first port of call,' said Macleod, 'Mairi Nicholson.'

'I was thinking whether or not he actually had a wife.'

'He does,' said Macleod. 'It's on his record. Ross could pick that up. He's going over that way this afternoon. In fact, he should be there by now, moved on from finding Carmichael's body. I take it that forensics have checked in with you on that one.'

'They're looking at it at the moment, inspector, but from what I hear, the man's been dead at least two to three weeks.'

'I thought as much because this lot had been here on the rig. That would have been done when they were back off on land. We're going to need to trace them on their travels. Get Ross on CCTV around the ferry ports and check the planes. I still

113

don't know why they're doing it, Jona, but at least I can pin somebody down on opportunity, if not motive.'

There was a banging on the door. 'Inspector, inspector,' came the voice. It was McCallan. Macleod turned to the door, pulling it open.

'What's up, man? What's the matter?'

'We've got your station on the line. Do you have an officer called Ross?'

'Yes. What's up with Ross? Does he need me?'

'There's been a fire, inspector. You need to come to the phone. There's been a fire.'

Chapter 14

Ross could feel the heat of the flames as they crept closer, the wood starting to burn in an uncontrollable blaze. He reached around him, desperately looking for something, anything. The smoke was now starting to fill the inside as well. As soon as his head left the floor from where he'd been sucking the clean oxygen, he got up into blinding flurry of smoke that choked him. His hand swung out, looking for the tools he'd photographed earlier. His hand grabbed something. He wasn't quite sure what it was, but it was metal and had a sharp edge on it as his hand cut across it. Falling back to the floor, choking as he did, Ross shuffled until his head banged on the wall of the shed. There, he took the implement and drove it several times at the base of the shed.

'Come on, Alan, you need this. Come on.' Before him, Ross could see the face of his partner, could see the life that was going to dwindle away from him. 'No,' he said, coughing and spluttering and sweating due to a mix of the heat within the shed and the effort to try and drive the implement in his hands through the wall. He felt it go through once, cutting a small hole. Then he felt it again. The fire was continuing to rage, possibly up and over him by now, but it was coming along through the walls as well. He stuck his mouth to the hole he had created and drew in breath of what felt like cleaner air. Having done so, he drove again with the implement right beside where he already created a hole.

Desperately, he started to try and shake through the hole, but the smoke made him cough and splutter. Instead, he decided to renew his efforts with the tool in his hand before the oxygen would be starved from him and he could no longer force his way out. The hole grew slightly bigger and he could get an arm out now. He could feel the wood starting to waver and so spun himself around and kicked as hard as he could. The wood splintered as he felt his jacket go on fire. His feet now emerged from the shed, and he pushed as hard as he could with flames all around him. Dragging himself out of the hole, Ross rolled, finding grass, and spun over and over again.

Standing up, he tried to unzip his jacket, but his hands were scalded by the zip. Instead, he drove himself back to the ground, rolling again until all the flames were out; then he collapsed on the ground, sucking in lungfuls of air. Ross wasn't sure how long he was laying there, but the shed continued to blaze. Eventually, he reached down into his pocket to find his mobile phone. It was still active with a weak signal. He pressed the button for the station switchboard. Through coughing splutters, he managed to detail the situation before he collapsed back down again and tried to suck in more air.

Ross wasn't sure if he passed out or not. The next thing he remembered was hearing the sirens, and the same police officers he'd been with that day were now turning up to help him. Not long after, an ambulance arrived and the paramedics took him inside the vehicle, checking him over. When they insisted that Ross had to go to a hospital to be checked over, he took one of the police sergeants to one side and detailed how he wanted the building to be searched. He gave a timeline of what had happened to him and what he had seen through the window. The camera was fortunately in his pocket and he handed it to the sergeant, asking him to get forensics to take a look at it.

With an oxygen mask over his mouth, Ross's last effort was to try to call Macleod. The paramedics wouldn't have it and laid him down and told him to rest. As he disappeared off to Raigmore Hospital just across from the Inverness Station, Ross drifted off to sleep. He hadn't called Macleod. That was all that went through his head before sleep overtook him.

* * *

Kirsten Stewart was sitting in the South Beach bar. In Scotland, they called it a spit and sawdust pub, one which men would normally frequent, although these days, you could get quite a few women in as well. But it was no classy joint. If anything, it was the bottom rung, and Stewart could certainly attest to this. She was sitting in a corner with a lemonade in front of her and had insisted on a slice of lemon in it, to make it out it was a G and T. Still, this was not a pub for gin and tonic. As she was sitting there, her mobile began to vibrate, and pulling it out , she saw the frosty stares of the locals.

The text she received simply said, 'Ross in a fire, off to hospital, call in.' When Kirsten went to slide out from the wooden seat she was on to make her way outside and call the station, a girl sat down opposite her.

'Who are you?' said the dark-haired girl. Kirsten guessed she was at best early twenties, possibly younger, but she wore black jeans and a black jacket, which was laid open on a tight top showing ample cleavage, which stared back at Kirsten.

'I'm just someone sitting having a drink,' said Kirsten. 'What's it to you?'

'They say you're a copper, say you're police. Is that right?'

'What's it to you if I am?'

'Said you're looking for Angus Macleod. Somebody said he died out in the rig.'

'What if he did?'

'Well, Angus owes me money, so I'd like to get it back. It doesn't really work if he's dead.'

'I guess it doesn't. What does he owe you money for?'

'Looking after his needs,' said the girl, 'if you catch my drift.' Kirsten looked at the girl. She caught her drift straight away. 'I think you're going to struggle for your money,' said Kirsten. 'Dead men don't pay well.'

'No, they don't, but I thought you might,' said the girl. 'You might want to know a little bit about him. I could probably tell you about his movements. You see, he's been seeing me or rather, I've been seeing him, so I can tell you when he's been about.'

Kirsten looked past the girl and saw a man in the corner of the pub looking over at them. This wasn't overly unusual as most of the locals were turning around and staring at Kirsten on and off, but this man seemed bothered. 'Who's the guy at the back?' asked Kirsten.

The girl looked around and was visibly shocked. 'Bloody hell; trust him to be bloody in here. That's my dad.'

'Does he know that you—'

'Like he gives a damn. Tries to get money off me all the time— come in here and pisses it away. He's done sod all for

118

me. Do you know that? Sod all. I only do this because Mum died. She died and he was meant to look after me. Got no schooling; had to look after him instead. Nights sat on the sofa, pissed out of his head. What do you do when you've got no qualifications? What do you do when you haven't had schooling, instead having to look after someone else? Anyway, what's that to you? You want to know about Angus or not?'

'I want to know all about Angus,' said Stewart. 'I can't pay you.'

'Even if it's good?'

'I take it this is off the record,' said Kirsten.

'Do you really think I'm going to sit here and tell you about how I've been a prostitute, how I've been earning cash illegally? You say anything else, I'll deny it and you can't tape me without telling me.'

'I'm not concerned about taping you. I'm not concerned about booking you or anything like that. I just want to know what you know. Man's been murdered. You've just told me you've been with him a lot. You need to tell me what you know.'

'Okay, but this is worth it. This is worth a hundred. Do you understand me? You bring me in, I'll clam up; I'll say nothing. He died in an oil rig. It wasn't me. I've been here, but I want a hundred for what I've got.'

'Tell me what you've got, then I'll give you the hundred,' said Stewart.

The girl stared at Stewart, questioning whether she was genuine. Stewart reached inside her pocket and pulled out a number of notes, holding them in her hand. The girl nodded.

'The thing about Angus was he was going to come into some money, or at least I think he had come into some money.'

'What do you mean?' asked Stewart.

'He started looking to buy things. You've got to understand, Angus lived in a shit hole. He never bought anything. It was all second hand, rubbish. He never had any cash. He'd been after me for ages. You see, I knew him at school. He knew me as well, always had an eye for me, and then when I got into this line of work, he had asked me several times, and I told him, "No, you can't afford me." To be honest, I didn't want to be afforded by him, so I told him a price that was five times what I actually charge. Well, lo and behold, recently, he turns up and says, "I can pay you that." I wasn't keen, but I couldn't turn down money like that. That piss head back over at the bar, saw to that. He goes to a night of gambling, ran up debts, then people came looking for him, so I needed the money. You know what; he didn't last that long anyway.'

Kirsten raised the glass to her mouth, drinking down some of her lemonade. The information was good, but the image being painted was gross in the extreme. Kirsten hadn't grown up amongst this sort of life and she'd always wondered where these people existed. Now she was in the force, she was finding them more and more common than she'd ever hoped. 'Do you know where the money came from?'

'No, I don't,' said the girl. 'I'll tell you this. Three times I was in, he had this painting on the wall. He's never had a painting on the wall in his life. The first time we're in his bedroom, he had pictures, all right, but they weren't artistic. Well, maybe some people would say they're artistic, but the sort of artistic stuff you get on a top-shelf, but this one, this was a naked woman. But it was proper painted, done by somebody fancy, no doubt. It was up there for three visits that I did with him, and then it was gone. Then another one turns up, different subject matter though. He didn't have these things. Why were they hanging on his wall? Anyway, as I said, he's got all this money and he's paying me and he says he's going to be able to pay me so much so that he actually said to me at one point, "Was I interested in being more than just someone he paid money to? Was I interested in being his little woman as he put it?" Well, I wasn't. I don't care how much money he's got. The guy was a slime ball. Then he was off to the rig, so I haven't seen him for a while.'

'When you say he was coming into the money, how much money?'

'He was talking like he'd be set up for life. He kept saying to me, 'Soon I'll be able to buy this, I'll be able to buy that. I'm not able to get too much at the moment. It's not time yet,' he's saying. He said these were only down payments that he had. That's why he was spending it on what he really wanted, which unfortunately meant me.'

'Anything else?' asked Stewart.

'No,' said the girl. 'No. I was with him; he paid me. He was into a lot of money. Other than a couple of paintings he had, I couldn't tell you anything else because I got in there, I did what I had to do for him, and I got out. Like I said, I wasn't interested in him. I don't care how much money he's got. I just wanted enough to keep Dad safe, to stop him getting his legs broke by people he owed money to.'

'Is your dad a junkie?' asked Stewart.

'Plain and obvious, isn't it? Total junkie. How did I end up with him? Anyway, give us the money. I told you what I know.'

Stewart raised her hand and placed the money in front of the girl, who grabbed it quickly, tucking it away inside her top. Without a word, she turned and left the bar, leaving Stewart on her own. She drank the last of her lemonade and stood up to be followed across the bar, eyes looking here and there. Stepping out into the daylight, her eyes adjusting to the sun, Kirsten began to phone the station with her mobile, but something caught her eye across the small square. She was sure she was looking at the man she had chased at the model aircraft club.

Quickly, she stepped to one side into an alley and looked around to see the man start to walk after someone. He was moving in a quick but careful fashion. Stewart decided to tail him. She followed him into the centre of Stornoway, then up past a church and into some residential streets further away from the centre of the town. *He seems incredibly focused on what is ahead of him*, Stewart thought; *tailing him is far too easy*. After a moment, he began to run. Stewart followed him, keeping at a distance but never losing touch. As he came to the rear of a school, she saw the man running to a hedge at the rear of a building. Stewart maintained her pursuit, and then heard a sharp cry from a girl. As she got closer, she recognized the young woman who she'd just given money to in the bar.

The man had clearly punched the girl, and as he was grabbing her, arm around her throat, she was beginning to choke. The girl looked like she wanted to scream, but the air had been taken out of her. All she could do was wave her arms around ineffectually. She tried to grab the man's hair, tried to pull at him, but nothing was stopping his grip.

Stewart yelled, 'Stop. Police,' and ran hard towards the fighting couple. The man looked around, sweat across his face, weighed up his options and roughly deposited the girl on the ground before sprinting off. Stewart looked at him, but her first duty was to the girl and running up to her, she saw she was lying motionless on the ground. Stewart turned the girl onto her back, and breathed a sigh of relief when the eyes opened. The girl tried to speak, but she couldn't. She spluttered, coughing.

'Take it easy,' said Stewart. 'He's gone. I've chased him off. He's gone.' It took a moment for the girl to recover, for Stewart to pull her up so she was in a sitting position. Around her neck were deep red marks and Stewart swore she would come out in a bruise. 'First of all, you need to tell me your name, and you need to tell me why he is after you.'

'I'm Anna, Anna McQuinn, and I've never seen that flaming guy before in my life.'

'Did he say anything to you? Did he ask you anything?'

'All he said was, "Why are you talking to that copper? What did you tell that copper?"'

'What did you say to him?'

The girl coughed again, spitting the phlegm onto the ground in front of Stewart. 'I told him jack. He wasn't offering any money like you were.' With that, the girl reached inside her top, removing the money, handing it back to Stewart. 'I guess I owe you this for saving my life.'

Stewart pushed the money back to her. 'You can keep it, love. I think you need it. It's my job. This is what I do, so I don't want payment for it, but we need to get you to the hospital, and I need you to make a statement for me.'

The girl looked up and started standing upright. She was shaking, wobbly, but she was determined to get there. 'Look, no statements. I told you what I know. I don't stand around in the limelight here. It's not good for business. It's not good for me. The last thing I need is to be associated with you if arseholes like that are going to come and do this to me. No offence, love. Thanks for helping me, but you can piss off with the statement.'

The girl began to walk away. At first, Stewart thought she should go after her, but she could always get her again. She knew her face, she knew her name, and she knew what she did. The girl had just given her another possible line of inquiry, and then Stewart's mind clicked back into focus. Ross. They had said something was up with Ross. She grabbed her mobile again.

Chapter 15

Macleod sat across from a dark-haired man in his mid-thirties. He recognized the Lewis twang in the man's accent when he originally asked him his name. Other than that, DJ Macleod had said very little. There'd been a gruff, 'Yes' when Macleod had asked him to confirm his movements, detailing them for the man.

'What you didn't tell me was that you knew Mairi Nicholson, very well. Girl of yours at school. That's what I heard.'

The man's eyes shifted here and there as if looking for a way out of the room. He gave a small cough, but Macleod could see the discomfort underneath.

'Yes, I did. I knew Mairi, but we don't tend to talk about that.'

'Why is that then?' asked Macleod.

'Well, she got involved with her teacher.'

'I heard you were all involved with that teacher in some degree.' The man's face looked shocked.

'Wasn't like that. None of the rest of us had anything sexual with him. He just hung out with us. We were of an age when he could get us things, Mr Carmichael, but all he wanted was Mairi.'

'Did that anger you?' asked Macleod. 'I mean, did that really get under your skin?'

Macleod saw the man's eyes shift uneasily again. 'It did, Inspector. If you must know, it did. It always has done. It still does. What else would you like me to say?'

'I'd like you to say where you were over the last three weeks before you were on this oil rig. We found Mr Carmichael. He's dead. You see, I've got three bodies. Angus Macleod, who I believe was part of your little group at school. Younger than most of you, but still there at the same time, and I believe still hung around with you. Alastair Nicholson, face battered in, so bad you can't recognize him. Another part of your group, Mairi's brother. Then there's Mr Carmichael. From nowhere, suddenly he's dead. He's been found in a caravan, about a mile away from a house where an officer of mine has just been burnt.'

Macleod saw the man's shocked face. 'Yes, that's right, somebody tried to kill one of my own, so you can imagine I'm not very happy at the moment, Mr Macleod. Kindly tell me everything from the top. Tell me about you as a group.'

'Now hang on a minute. You can't blame that on me. I didn't do that. I'm on the rig. How can I set fire to something, attack your officer when I'm on the rig?'

'Well, somebody is doing something,' said Macleod, 'because I've got two officers. One is being followed. The other's attacked in completely different places. This smacks of a large group working together and I've got a large group who knew Angus Macleod, and a relationship between you and Mairi Nicholson, and a former teacher is at the centre of it. I want to know everything. I want to know your movements for the last three months.'

126

The man stayed silent. 'Did you not hear me? I said I wanted to know your movements for the last three months. When was the last time you saw Mairi Nicholson off this rig? When was the last time you saw Alastair Nicholson off this rig, and your two Macleod cohorts as well, Ian and James— when did you see them?'

'I've seen them in passing at times. I mean we all live in Stornoway. Well, Alastair didn't. Alastair moved away a while ago. I knew Alastair did quite well for himself.'

'From the house my officer was at, he did very well for himself. Too well. Not well enough for what you earn on this rig. How does he have a house that big? Do you know?'

'He married well, Inspector. Some posh bird. Never met her, but Mairi told me when I met her in town. Always on about how her brother had done so well.'

'Yet he's here lying on a table with his face bashed in,' said Macleod. 'Why is that? Why was Angus Macleod killed, and then hung up to make it look like a suicide?'

'Look, I told you. When we were at school, I was with Mairi. Then she starts telling me that Carmichael can get us stuff. You know, alcohol, even some drugs and things. I was pals with Ian and James. James would bring Angus along. Alastair was younger than Mairi, closer to Angus's age. We'd all been in primary school together as well, so we knew each other. Then we'd head up into the back of the castle grounds. That's the castle up in Stornoway. Lots of people used to go up in there.'

'I'm from Lewis and I know it well. I know the sort of people that used to go up there. How often did you do this?'

'A year before our finals. There was a bit of a scandal with it. Carmichael lost his job. That never came out though. School kept it suppressed. The last thing they wanted. He wasn't doing anything illegal. Mairi was seventeen. The only thing they could have done him for was passing on the alcohol to Alastair or Angus. He could've blamed that on us anyway. They weren't really that involved. It was mainly us older ones that did it.'

Macleod sat back in his chair. He wasn't getting told anything that he didn't know. The story was the same. The only time they met these days was passing in town, seeing each other on the rig. There were nods, there were hellos, but that was it.

The story was the same when Macleod interviewed Ian Macleod and James Macleod. Each story exactly the same. In fact, too much the same. Every single one of them denying meeting with each other in any way except in town. They spoke of cars passing by, saying hello in the street. It riled Macleod. He could tell they were lying but he had no proof.

Retiring to the canteen, Macleod decided to try one last time with Mairi Nicholson. Before he could make his way, Hope cornered him in the cafeteria.

'I heard from the hospital. Ross is fine. He got some minor smoke inhalation; other than that, there's been nothing, no injuries. He got lucky. He said he was on the floor. Had to smash his way out.'

'They're lying in there. I don't know what about. I don't know why,' said Macleod. 'I heard from Stewart as well. She's got somebody on her tail, and this is what I don't get. Why? Why is this happening? Who are these other people who set the fire that nearly killed Ross? Who's tailing Stewart? We've got our suspects in the ring but there's a bigger thing going on here. We're missing the big picture.'

'We don't seem to have anybody else in the group from

Stornoway, the group that hung around in the school, the group that was with Carmichael. I ran through the school records again, asked them if there's anybody else involved in the Carmichael incident. They said, 'No.''

'In that case, Hope, there's another interested party. Something else. These guys aren't able to afford henchmen. Somebody else is doing this. We need to find out why.'

'Well, one thing I do know,' said Hope, 'Jona got some information back and she wants to speak to us. Before you go and see Mairi Nicholson, I suggest you hear her out.'

'We better be quick,' said Macleod. 'Tomorrow, these guys leave the rig, and I can't hold them. I've got nothing to charge them with.'

'I'll go get Jona now. Where do you want to do this? In your room?'

Macleod nodded. 'Yes. We're going to keep it tight whatever it is she knows. I'm telling you, Hope, there's more involved in this. This is wider. There are other parties involved. This group has a secret, something they're holding back. Something that may have gone wrong. Otherwise, why are two of them dead? I'll see you in five minutes in mine, with Jona.'

Macleod sipped his coffee and then wearily made his way back to his room. He found Hope and Jona already outside, so unlocked the door and, together, they made their way in. Being the gentleman he'd been brought up to be, Macleod stood while the women sat down on the chairs beside the table.

'What have you got, Jona?'

'Inspector, we got word about the photographs that Ross took and the ones he shot through the curtain at the house. It is very indistinct but we managed to enhance them. One of the guys in the lab recognized the house by the way, because he'd been over there for a tour. It's owned by a Lord, Lord Argyll, and it stocks a rather fine collection of artwork. Here's the thing. It stopped doing guided tours about two months ago. Nobody seems to be able to find out why.

We know through the windows of the rest of the house that Ross said there was lots of artwork; there were auction catalogs, things like that. The house that Ross was at belongs to Alastair Nicholson and his wife, Gemma. We managed to contact her. She's coming back. Hope believes Ross is going to organize some of your uniforms to go down and interview her, if not himself. She seems quite shocked but apparently, she's the one in the know about the artwork. She has a bit of a reputation along those lines.

'Where did we get all the information from? Have we got anybody on our side who understands this world?' said Macleod. 'Because quite frankly, you're moving into stolen items that I have no idea about. Things that I wouldn't know the value of, how easy to access, how easy to shift on. See, if you can tag me in with somebody on that side, Jona.'

'Will do, Inspector,' said Jona, 'But like I say, I think Ross has got to head over to the Lord Argyll's residence tomorrow. He's looking for a good night's sleep tonight.' Macleod nodded.

'I'll get Mairi Nicholson set up for your interview?' asked Hope.

'I'll be two minutes,' said Macleod. 'See you in there.' With that, Hope left the room but Macleod stopped Jona before she departed. 'Remind me again,' said Macleod, 'when Nicholson was killed, it was quite brutal, wasn't it?'

'Very, almost like out of control,' said Jona.

'That's in contrast to what happened with Angus. Plan's

possibly gone awry, and they managed to hang him up in the kitchen. Cool and calm thinking, wouldn't you say?'

'I find it hard to disagree with you, Seoras, but I wouldn't want to say for definite that there were different people. The way people react is different. Maybe the victim caused them to react this way or that way. Maybe there was more of a struggle.'

'Agreed,' said Macleod, 'but they're different in the murder style; that's possibly two different killers. Just something to think about. When you get better forensics on our friend down in the caravan, Mr Carmichael, let me know.'

'Will do, Seoras. What are you going to do about them leaving tomorrow? You going to keep them here on the rig?'

'I can't. I don't have anything to charge them with, Jona. Unless you're going to come up with something special, they're going back to the mainland. But if they do, I'm going to make sure we've got eyes on them.

The diminutive Asian woman left and Macleod pulled himself from the wall he was leaning on. He was dog-tired. Dog-tired and had nothing to show for it. Maybe Mairi Nicolson would come up with something.

As Macleod entered the room, he saw Mairi Nicolson sitting tidily behind the desk. Long black hair in ringlets were flowing down her back, but her eyes were showing steel. Hope sat opposite her in a very calm and detached fashion, something Macleod was becoming to admire in his partner. She had grown as an officer, grown as a detective, learning more and more when to cover her hand.

'Why am I in here? My brother's dead. Somebody beat my brother to death, and you have me in here.'

'You're in here because you don't tell me the truth. You told me you didn't really know any of these people, the Macleods. You didn't even mention the fact that Alastair was your brother. What do you expect me to do? Somebody doesn't tell me things up front, without me having to dig, I go on and ask them some more— seems only fair.'

Macleod watched the woman tut. She shook her head. 'It's that whole Carmichael incident, isn't it? It's the whole Carmichael incident, just coming up again. I'm sick of it. I'm bloody sick of it. I did nothing wrong back then, nothing at all and yet you're hounding me. It's time you guys left me alone. I've got enough to mourn now.'

'Have you contacted Gemma?' Mairi's eyes rolled. She looked angry. 'We don't talk to her,' she said. 'I've never been interested in talking to her.'

'So that's a no?' said Hope. 'You haven't been in touch?'

'Why would I? I'm sure you guys have told her. Let her know that Alastair's dead?'

'Somebody else has been around Alastair's house. One of our colleagues was nearly burnt to death in a fire at your brother's house.' Macleod saw the reaction. It was very controlled, but that brief moment when she started. 'Well, that's her business, isn't it? Wasn't me that did that; you can't blame me. I was on the rig.'

'I didn't say I was blaming you,' said Macleod. 'I'm looking at you for what happened to Carmichael.'

There was a flinch, but this time Macleod thought it was too much. Was that an over-reaction? A forced one, a pretend one? 'Been years since I've seen Carmichael, but what he did to me, good riddance. Promised me the earth, he did. Promised me riches.'

'So, what, you went to bed with him for riches?' said Hope.

'Were you really that naïve at seventeen?'

Mairi Nicholson said nothing, but her eyes sparked fire at Hope. *Oh yes*, thought Macleod, *Hope said something there*.

'Can you tell me anything else about your relationship with Mr Carmichael? I've heard plenty about it, from DJ, Ian, and James. Said you were in love with him. Is that the case or were you just playing?'

'I was seventeen; what did you expect?' But Macleod looked into the eyes of Mairi Nicholson and saw something. There was a pain there, a hunger, an anger. Maybe she had expected more. 'But it ain't something I'm talking about. I told you what I've told you, that I haven't seen him in years. If you let me go, I'm off here tomorrow. That's unless you intend to keep us captive.'

'You'll be free to go tomorrow,' said Macleod. 'But don't leave the country. I believe you're all going back to Stornoway. Is that the case? Maybe you'll be feeling the need to go and see Gemma, offer your sister-in-law some comforting arms now that she's a widow.'

'Am I done here? If you don't mind, I'd like to be on my own.'

Macleod turned and stared at Hope, but his decision was already made. 'We'll talk again Mairi. Probably in Stornoway though.' With that, Macleod stood up and exited the room.

Chapter 16

Macleod watched the helicopter lift, aware that all of his suspects were on board. The wheels gently took off, the helicopter seemed to wave in the air, and then it powered up, lifting, moving forward at the same time. Within a couple of minutes, it was disappearing out of sight. Macleod was himself scheduled on another helicopter in about three hours' time. He left Hope assisting Jona with packing up the forensic gear. Beside him stood David McCallan, the platform manager who was shaking his head.

'Good riddance; time to get back to some normality around here.'

'You might be called on again,' said Macleod, 'especially when this goes to court. You'll be asked to say what happened. Not that I think any of it has got anything to do with you, sir. Just be aware of that. Don't broadcast opinions, or your views, or anything like that. No doubt, your bosses will want a report. Be very factual, straightforward. I think that always goes down best.'

'I'll bear that in mind, inspector.'

'The Macleods have just left and Mairi Nicholson. How did

you find them on the platform? Did you ever see much of them?'

'A lot of the people here are just names for me. I'll tell you that. Andrea might know more. I guess you've already spoken to her.'

'Not in the depth I'd want to,' said Macleod.

'Just hang here. I'll get her to come see you. If you stay up here, you'll be out of earshot of most people.' Macleod stood in what was a brisk breeze, hearing the crashing sea below him until Andrea Romain pitched up beside him. She was wearing a hard hat, hair tied up behind her. Macleod wondered if he looked as stupid in his hard hat as he thought she did. It was the way things always sat off your head, not like a proper hat.

'Inspector, David said you wanted to see me.'

'That's right, Miss Romain. Thanks for coming to see me. It's just Mairi Nicholson and the Macleods have disappeared off— DJ, Ian, and James. Did you have much contact with them? Did they ever come to you for much?'

'Not really. Mairi did once or twice looking for shift swaps. There was a couple of times we tried to reschedule her, but she was adamant. She couldn't come out here except at those times. When I pushed on it, it was always something medical, hard things to go into to investigate. She was always keen to be here at certain times.'

'With the rest of the guys, did your rosters ever get skewed? Were any of them ever having to come out or ask to change?'

'No,' said Andrea, 'But then again, they all work in a similar place. As I recall, they are on a fairly similar rotation. There's only Mairi who ever would be anything different. We looked to switch her over because of female accommodation and with her technician job. She wasn't some specialist that we needed her specifically.'

'Okay, so you would say that she actually actively tried to be on at the same time as the rest of them?'

'I can't say that,' said Andrea. 'All I know is when we tried to change her or move her about, she didn't have it. She came up with all the different excuses, ones we couldn't get past. Like I say, when suddenly you're talking medical unless you have an incredibly good reason, you don't argue much with it.'

'Did you ever see any documentation?'

'No. I don't see the point if somebody is asking in that way. It wasn't like they were claiming money or anything. It's just trying to work the shift pattern.'

'That's understood. Thank you. You've been very helpful.' With that, Andrea Romain turned away leaving Macleod standing high above the sea.

He picked up his phone and placed a call through the WiFi to Ross. The constable answered it quickly and Macleod could hear the sound of a car in the background.

'Just let me pull over, sir. I'm on my way to Aberdeen.' Macleod waited until he heard the engine stop.

'You okay, Alan. I was told it was touch-and-go.'

'I just got a little bit of smoke inhalation. They say I'm fine. No damage, nothing burned. I was fortunate though, sir. There were some tools I managed to work my way out with. It seems crazy. I don't know what it is I'm meant to have seen. I also didn't know he was following me because frankly, I didn't see anyone. I was popping to the house just to take a scan around it. I wasn't looking to go inside. I didn't know nobody would be in. If it had happened over Carmichael's body, I could have understood it, trying to stop me producing evidence.'

'When you looked inside, they told me that you saw lots of auction house material, brochures, things like that and you photographed it. Jona said you then had to photograph through a net curtain into a second part of a study.'

'That's correct, boss. Everything in the house was quite easy to see into. You could walk up, peer in. One particular room had like a net curtain down in front of it that distorted everything, making it very hard to see. There seemed to be one important set of documents and photographs. A large picture of a house. I photographed it. The guys back in the lab came up with a name for the house. Lord Argyle's over in Aberdeen. That's where I'm on my way now, sir.'

'When you looked at the setup through the net curtain, did it look like a planning room? Did it look like there was a focus?'

'I would say so but couldn't guarantee it. No evidence in that sense. I must have seen something. Why else try and kill me? We're used to people coming in and stalling and diverting us but why kill? I didn't know anything.'

'No, but your camera may have. Get over to Lord Argyle's house, find out what it is, find out what he's got worth taking. I said earlier today to Hope that there's more than one set of parties involved here. We've got this crowd from Stornoway, the Macleods, and the Nicholsons, two dead here on rig. I reckon they've all been in cahoots about something. I think things are going sour. We're going to keep tabs on them as they've just departed in the helicopter back for the mainland. I'm coming over to join you.

'I want you to find out what's going on in that house. I reckon somebody's got a reason to be involved. They don't want anyone else to know. Also, you might get a call from someone from the force that Jona's searching up. We're starting to look into the auction houses and places like that. We need a bit of background and someone who understands the business. Jona is bringing someone in for us. If I'm not back, I've asked her to direct that person to you. I hope you're good with that, Ross. It's great to hear you're okay. Watch your back on this one.'

'I'm aware of that now sir, and she's been in contact— the art officer as they called her.'

Macleod closed the call and realized he was twiddling his thumbs again. He'd call back to Stewart soon to find out what she was doing. He was aware she was going to start going to the houses of the suspects, go and ask the neighbours what was going on. On the other hand, he felt better if she didn't, better if she kept her distance until the oil workers arrived. She'd have her work cut out soon enough.

* * *

Kirsten Stewart lay in the bath allowing the water to soak around her. She was usually one for a shower, but today for some reason she was feeling down. They told her about her brother, about the fact he'd gone downhill. Now they were looking after him. Maybe it was just a little blip on his road. Maybe he would get back up to a point where she could look after him, but she wasn't hopeful.

Kirsten was aware her life was maybe about to change. She was on the cusp of being alone in the house. The last few years she'd done her best to look after her brother, make time for him, be around him. It cost her in terms of her personal life. She hadn't had a boyfriend for years. There had been those who asked, but she'd been dedicated to her brother and to her job. She was grateful for the inspector taking her on, moving forward, giving her a chance to do so many different things after their initial meeting in Lewis. Here she was back again, searching something else out for him, ready to go into battle. She was struggling to get her heart into it despite the fact that she twice had to run down the same individual. He was bothering her. Her mind coming back to who on earth he was. Outside of that, she felt a glumness.

Stepping out of the bath, Kirsten dried herself down before making her way to the mirror in her hotel room. She stood before it, looking at herself. She was in good shape, physically fit. Mentally, she was sharp, and yet she felt this emptiness. She did enjoy working with the team and the boss had taken an interest in her. The man was clever, read people so well, and yet, Ross had said she was like him. Like Macleod, she had an instinct for people. She could also do the dog work, get down and dig things out.

Stewart was also coming to the point where she was starting to think about her sergeant's exam to see if she could step up the rank. In truth, if she did that, she wondered if she would still be on the same team? Hope wasn't going to go anywhere. She'd moved with Macleod too much and had ample opportunity to disappear. Now with this new boyfriend in Inverness, she was going to be in Stewart's way, unless Macleod retired. He wouldn't retire though, not until they pensioned him off. He had that hunger deep inside.

No, she thought, *It's not a hunger— it's a duty*. Stewart got that. She understood; that's why she was doing what she was doing. She could have quit and looked after her brother much more, but no, somebody had to stand up. As she wrapped the towel back around herself, she made her way over to the window.

Then there was the man. The man who had spoken to her in the hospital, when they were all waiting for Ross. She'd been in Raigmore hospital after Ross had been shot on the Monarch Isles. As she drank her coffee downstairs, the man from the security services, the ones people don't talk about, had approached her. It would be different. It might be something.

Stewart's mobile phone began to ring. She turned around, picked it up and realized it was the number of her brother's doctor. The conversation was brief. It seemed he was going downhill fast. The doctor reckoned he may not even know her the next time she was over. Stewart was polite. She asked pertinent questions. 'Would he still be okay physically, even though mentally he was far gone?' The doctor said they'd look after him. He would get the care that's needed to live out the rest of his life, however long that would be. The doctor reckoned it was at most five or six years. Kirsten thanked him and closed the call.

The world had just collapsed. The sky had fallen down, and yet, she'd seen it coming. That was the thing, no matter how much you prepare, when the thing actually happens, when the world does come apart, the raw pain is still there. She sat on the end of the bed, placed her head in her hands, and wept.

Chapter 17

Ross was approximately half a mile from Lord Argyle's residence. He had been intending to go straight there but a phone call had diverted him to a small country park. As he sat with a coffee in his car, he awaited the arrival of a colleague from the force, one he had never met before. She would be there in a Jaguar, he had been told by the station and he was to expect her within the hour. Ross asked her name and was told Clarissa Urquhart, a name he'd never heard of before. However, since he may be dealing with the art world, Ross was ready for any help he could receive. One of his great qualities was his ability to get on with anyone. He certainly felt no apprehension at the thought of a new colleague arriving.

The day was cloudy, and while not cold, you certainly required a jacket. He stood outside his car, his backside resting on the bonnet, and kept staring at any new arrivals into the park. There was the odd dog walker, an occasional family with a small child who went off walking, but it took the full hour before he saw a Jaguar drive in. The car pulled up in front of him, coming to a halt with a screech. The vehicle itself was an older model. Looking inside, he saw a woman staring back at him with sunglasses on. She had a scarf tied around her head and wore an immaculate jacket over a blouse. When she stepped out of the car, Ross saw the high heels and the tight skirt, but he was also struck by how the woman carried herself. Walking around the car, she extended a hand towards Ross and he found it was gloved.

'Good afternoon, Detective Constable Ross. I suppose I'm technically Sergeant Clarissa Urquhart, but most people call me Urquhart, as we just don't use the titles within our department.'

'What department is that?' asked Ross.

'I deal with the art thefts mainly. Working into that side of the world. Anything that involves a serious amount of money. Been brought up to it, you see. Been doing it with the family before I got involved with the police. Father always said it was the better side of the force to be in, a little bit of class, but he was a total prick, of course.'

Ross didn't know whether to laugh or simply nod in agreement. Despite his usual wit and warmth, he found himself slightly nervous around the woman.

He placed her in her mid-forties, and while she certainly had shape, she was no model figure. Instead, she had a large frame, but Ross reckoned she could certainly outrun himself, and most definitely the Inspector. Stewart and Hope had that fitness look about them, women who had been training, but Urquhart didn't. She was more refined, classier.

'If you don't mind, Alan, isn't it? I'd rather you get changed before we go up here. I thought rather than pitch up as two detectives or police officers looking for something, we should try and get in where we can see things properly.'

'How are you expecting us to do that?' asked Ross.

'I do have a persona that I use. Let's me get in to see some artwork that you really shouldn't be seeing. We've had tabs on Lord Argyle for a while. He said he has a rather unique collection hidden away. You don't get to see it normally, but I can get us in. He's not there at the moment, but I'm interested in making a bid on certain pieces he has. He's rather proud of them; that's why he's showing them to me. Vanity is such a sin, Alan. I don't think he'll sell, but I'm not going to let him know that either.'

Ross stared at the woman, unsure whether to believe she was for real. She certainly carried off the act.

'Be a sport, Alan. I think there's male facilities over there. I've picked out this suit for you, little cravat, and that. If you can pop that on and get back in the car, we'll get over there.'

'Is this your own Jag?'

'Yes, it is, Alan. It's rather good, isn't it? I like it.'

'I prefer to be called Ross. It's just a thing I have. I know the new names and that came out.'

'No, you'll be Als or Alan. Need to have the idea that we're friends, close ones.'

'I don't always come across that well— being the partner of a woman. It's not my cup of tea. I'm afraid I prefer men.'

'All the better; still Als though. I think you've got the look for it. You pop and get changed and we'll get on our way.'

Ross felt like he was being railroaded, not getting a say in anything he was doing, but he had asked for an art expert. Someone who knew the field, and Jona had said this woman was the person to go to.

Ross emerged looking immaculate with a white blazer with a large cravat, and a pair of slacks that he believed he couldn't have afforded in a million years. It wasn't his style and he felt he was at some sort of murder mystery night where he was playing the lord of the land.

'Try not to say much,' said Clarissa. 'Let me do the talking. Don't offer an opinion. Nod in agreement with me. Say yes. If you're really struggling, say, "I'm not so convinced," something like that. Don't make a direct statement about anything. We're going to look at pieces and we're looking at things that shouldn't be on display. He's going to want to know that we're for real. I am for real, Alan. I understand the art that we're going to see. You will be clueless. That's fine because I'm there. I'll cover your back. If he does ask a direct question, just look to me. Something like, "What would you say Clarissa?" I'll take the lead as the dominant side of the partnership.'

Ross could believe that. He simply nodded and made his way to the Jag, sliding into the passenger seat. Clarissa took the wheel, turned on the car, and drove rather sleekly out of the car park. As she hit the main road, Ross noticed she was at least twenty miles above the speed limit.

'Do you not think you should take it a bit steadier, being an officer and that?'

'Quite to the contrary, old sport. I think we shouldn't. I think we should arrive like we own the place. Who's to say they're not watching? I haven't been tailed to here, but as we get closer, they'll be eyes on. I have a persona. I'm not 'in' in this world. He doesn't know me. He just knows of me; they'll be suspicious of everything. But trust me, Alan, you'll be just dandy.'

Clarissa drove the Jaguar through the main gates of what appeared to be a rather large estate. The main house was extremely impressive, sporting large pillars at the front. Clarissa pulled up directly in front of the main doors, beeping the horn loudly.

The front doors opened and a butler appeared making his way quickly down the steps. 'Forgive me, your Ladyship. I shall attend to your car immediately. If you would step inside, his Lordship's personal secretary is there.'

'Not your Ladyship,' said Clarissa. 'That would be overstating my title. Ms Urquhart will do when you announce us. Ms Urquhart and Mr Ross.'

The man was taken aback but nodded politely and took the keys off Clarissa before driving the Jaguar around to the side of the house. Clarissa led the way, walking forward in heels that Ross thought impossible to walk in. As they entered through the large doors, Ross found himself in a hallway with wood panelling on all sides. There were large portraits on the wall and he began to stare quite fixedly at them. He felt a dig in the ribs from Clarissa.

'Don't stare at the junk, love. We're here to meet a man, get your eyes down looking for him, not this tittle-tattle on the walls.'

Suitably rebuked, Ross put his hands behind his back and began rocking back and forward on his heels, trying to indicate he had an impatience to get on. A door at the side of the hallway suddenly opened and a man dressed in a rather dapper suit made his way overextending a hand to Clarissa.

'Delighted to have you here. His Lordship will be absolutely through the moon. My name's Giles. I'll be your guide today.'

'Splendid, Giles. Splendid. Now if you don't mind, we'd rather get on quickly with this. I have an urgent appointment so I'm afraid I can only spare the hour. So, if we go directly to the pieces that would be rather opportune.

The man nodded politely and advised that he would escort them and requested that they follow him directly. Ross found himself being led through several wood-panelled corridors, down some steps, and into a room with bookcases on all walls. The man stepped forward, pulled at a book, and one of the bookcases slid to one side. Ross tried not to look surprised and watched Clarissa simply wave her hands, declaring, 'Marvellous. Oh, that's just marvellous. Have one of them myself back at the family home.'

After going through the passage, they entered a rather large room with many pictures on the wall. There were all sorts of sizes and Ross reckoned they were from different eras. He began to stare intently at one picture after another, each lit from above by a soft light. When Giles had his back turned, Clarissa gave him an approving nod before directing him over to several pictures on the far side. 'If you could just give me a little detail on these, please, Giles. What sort of money is he looking for them?'

The conversation went right over Ross's head. Talk of artists and different museums and pieces. Histories were being spoken of, but he noted that Clarissa seemed more aware of the history of many of the pieces than Giles did. As Ross stood and looked at one particular portrait, Giles came up beside him.

'Quite exquisite, don't you think? How would you rate this one, sir?'

Ross shook his head. 'Not convinced. Wouldn't you agree, Clarissa?'

The woman was magnificent, taking up his line of attack and charging through the history of the piece, pointing out the flaws and the errors and what was wrong with it. The whole experience took less than half an hour and by the time they were escorted back out of the building, Ross was in a state of flux. He had no idea what they'd learnt. The Jaguar was brought round and Clarissa got behind the wheel again, waving frantically, as she drove the car out of the front drive.

As they made their way onto the road, Ross went to speak to her, but she put her hand up, 'Not now. Not now. We'll go somewhere first.' It took about an hour's drive before Clarissa pulled up on an estate placing the car inside an open garage. She stepped out, closed the metal door, and then began to route around in a number of trunks that were stored in the garage. Ross noticed that she pulled out a pair of jeans, a t-shirt, and a jumper, and without any embarrassment, she simply changed in front of him. Now dressed in trainers, she removed Ross's clothes from the boot of the car, turned her back, and advised him he should get changed as well. Once he was clothed, she led him through to another garage and they drove off in a small mini. After recovering Ross's car, they were sitting together in a café, but Ross noted that Clarissa had Earl Grey tea in front of her.

'Sorry to go through all that; at least I can talk a bit more professionally now. We've been tracing Lord Argyle's purchases and recently he's been putting a lot of feelers out for items, seeing where they were bought. What's bothered us about it is, he hasn't been looking to buy, he's just been asking the question. That's made me think that he's lost ownership of them. Having got in there today, I can tell you this, he has lost ownership. There's a collection of paintings there that I reckon there's at least four missing from. The hallway he's got them lined up on now, he wouldn't do that. They should be there as a set. Giles was trying to flog others off to me. He's checking to see if I've got the rest of the collection. Of course, I haven't, but they want to know who has. Somebody's been in there. Somebody's been in that estate, somebody's stolen his property. I'll make a note of what paintings, et cetera, you're looking for, and I'll get them over to you.'

'So, if they're stolen, why has he not said they were stolen?' asked Ross.

'Because he shouldn't have them in the first place, love,' said Clarissa.' He would have had to acquire them illegally. They went missing from a museum about six years ago. They've never been found and they've been passed on through different hands. He's had them. Most of that stuff in there he shouldn't have and at some point, we might come in and nail him for it, but in the meantime, we're going to exploit him. If I can get in, I might be able to get links of where the network is running. If we can bring down the network, it's much better than bringing down somebody like Lord Argyle.

'He's got money and he can get himself out of it. The fencers and the runners and everyone else, they won't be able to. That's how we close it down. But I hope I've assisted you. If you do find the pictures, the paintings, do let me know however I can be of further assistance. Pass on my regards to your Inspector Macleod.'

'I will do, and thank you,' said Ross. 'Do you know the inspector?'

'Only by reputation; sounds like my sort of man.'

Ross stepped up from his chair and left the café. As he turned to go for his car, he looked back in through the window and saw the woman delicately lifting her cup drinking her Earl Grey tea. *Remarkable*, he thought. *Just remarkable.*

Chapter 18

The ditch Kirsten Stewart was currently standing in was boggy, a product of the recent rain. April on the Isle of Lewis brought a mix of weather. Last night it had rained heavily, filling up the ditches that had been dry just the previous day. This particular ditch surrounded the house of James Macleod. Located on the edge of Stornoway, it stood a quarter of a mile away from the next house and was built on a piece of moorland where they had to build large ditches to the sides of the roads to allow for good drainage. Much of Lewis was a bog. So much so, that most of the houses were built to allow the wind to pass underneath and through the attic spaces to keep the buildings dry.

When Kirsten had first hired a house, she'd found this to her cost. Used to somewhere on the mainland with good cavity-wall installation and various other insulated areas, her house had been easy to heat, but here, they said that too well-sealed a house led to damp. That had been true in her rented accommodation. The air passed through so quickly, it was bone dry, but it was also so cold she'd wrapped herself up at night in blankets, pulling herself and her brother close to the stove in the main room.

Of course, she knew which type of house she would have preferred. Indeed, the new-builds on the island were following the well-insulated state of affairs, but the older houses still remained, and this looked like one of them. There were two large windows at the front to either side of a door with a small porch. Upstairs, she saw two more smaller windows and reckoned those rooms were built into the sloping roof. Maybe there wasn't much of an attic up above.

She knew James Macleod was back on the island, having waited at the house for most of the morning before spotting him. Her car was parked further down the road beside another house and while she would have preferred to be sitting in it, the distance and the contours of the land were too much for a clear view. So, she'd walked the quarter of a mile and positioned herself down low in a ditch, and was watching James with binoculars through a hedge. James was currently in the kitchen.

Kirsten would rather have been on the move hunting people down, rather than sitting doing observation, because the situation of her brother was playing on her mind. She tried to focus, tried to count various aspects of the house, tried peering in through the kitchen window to see exactly what James was doing. When she realized he was having a bowl of cornflakes, her perculiar game was up.

Kirsten was aware that Macleod was coming back that day. He'd be on the island soon enough. Even though he never said it, he would be demanding results with his manner. She liked that about him. Macleod was always fair, but firm. You just had to be careful you didn't get on the wrong side of him when things weren't going well. He got worked up, angry at times. Though he'd never lashed out, physically or verbally, she could see the rage inside him that he fought to control. He was also a bit staid in his views and opinions, but he stood up for his team and she certainly learned a lot from him.

Mind you, the amount of computer work she had done for him, she deserved a bit of backup. The man was a dinosaur when it came to technology.

Then she thought about another boss, a potential one. In her jacket pocket, there is a small piece of paper in which she'd written the name of the company the man worked for, but the name was just a front. Working for the services, the undercover ones, the ones the country didn't talk about; in a lot of ways, it was appealing to Kirsten. But she never would have given it a second thought. Not while she was looking after her brother. Now they were telling her he wasn't going to be right.

She would be lucky if he would recognize her. If she went visiting, would it still be for him? If he didn't know her, did it make a difference? They said he could have a life, but one day to the next, he wouldn't know who was who or what. The idea that one day he could be scared of her frightened Kirsten. She'd been a constant in his life, especially since their parents had died, but she'd always known his mind would get worse. Maybe it was time to start thinking about her. Maybe it was time to take this chance.

Truthfully, she wanted to speak to Macleod about it. She wanted to understand his views on it. He was someone she looked up to, someone whose opinion she treasured. She knew inside that when he congratulated her, when he told her she'd done something well, her heart leapt. The esteem with which she held him was more than she held for most people in her life but she couldn't talk to him about this, could she? He wouldn't want her to leave. He needed her too much. Hope will be the same.

Strictly, she should go to Hope as her line manager. As much as she had respect for her sergeant, they were not the same breed. They worked on different levels. That was good for the team, but not good for discussion about private life, about careers, and aspirations. Macleod was always easier to talk to about these things, though Ross disagreed, but then again, the boss didn't handle the whole LGBTQ thing. He tried, but it was quite clear; the old prejudices he'd been brought up with were still there, even if he didn't let them come out in his speech.

Kirsten caught herself daydreaming. There was a large knock at the door and she put the binoculars up to her eyes and saw a familiar face. She had chased him on several occasions and she wondered what he was doing here. So far, he seemed to be following her. She'd been on the lookout this time. The hire car, that she had parked at the house up the road was different. She had made sure her back was covered and she'd been in this ditch for an age, without a soul being anywhere near the house.

Kirsten tensed, wondering what the man would do. He had attacked Danielle MacIver, the woman who had given her so much information in the pub, but it seemed he hadn't known her; he was merely trying to question her after he saw her conversing with Kirsten. The Model Club incident had simply been the man tailing Stewart, but this was different. He was at one of the suspects' house and Stewart was sure he hadn't simply followed her there.

James Macleod looked anxious in the kitchen, as the door was rapped again. The man seemed to be pondering his next move, but slowly he turned and made his way out of the kitchen. The front door opened and she saw James Macleod standing there in a dressing gown, just a man who'd gone for a shower after arriving at the house, possibly after all the travel.

The man who seemed to be following Stewart everywhere was dressed in a black coat, black hat on but his face was distinct. He certainly wasn't smiling at this time, and the questions he asked seemed to catch James almost as if he'd been punched in the stomach. James said very little, and the man seemed displeased with this. When a hand shot out from him, grabbing James by the collar and dragging him out the front door, Stewart decided she needed to make a move.

Maybe it was the squelch that she made as she tried to clamber out of the ditch, but something alerted the man. As she made her way onto the road and started running for the house, Stewart saw the man slap James several times with the back of his hand, demanding to know something. The words were indistinct at this distance, but he clearly was intent on getting an answer before Stewart got there.

A second slap. James seemed to mutter something, but Stewart was now at the garden gate and about to enter the path down to the front door. She saw the man drop Macleod straight to the floor, and he turned, running off to the rear of the house. Stewart barked, 'Stay there,' at James Macleod and tore around the side of the house in pursuit of the man in black but she was too keen. As she turned a corner an arm came out, catching her full in the face. Her legs went from under, sweeping out in front, and she fell hard on her back.

Kirsten was prone on her back, and fully expecting the man to jump on top of her. She threw her arms in front of her, lifted her knees up in anticipation of him getting on top, bracing herself to push back but he simply ran off. *Not this time*, thought Stewart. *Not this time. This time I'm having you.*

She leapt up to her feet, seeing the man exit a gate through the rear garden, and out to the moorland behind. Stewart skipped along the side of the house down to the gate and then found her feet starting to squelch as she made her way out onto the wet moor.

Having been in Lewis before, she'd actually conducted several searches across moorland, and the one thing you began to learn was that the whole moor was not the same. If you were careful and watched the colour of the land and the type of foliage that was on it, you could see where your foot was going to sink further. The bog was not consistent. In patches, you might go down to your ankle, in other parts, it was as solid as pavement. As she watched the black-dressed man make his way across the moor, running as hard as he could, she recognized he was about to head for a large but soft patch of land.

Stewart cut a slightly different line, keeping up on the firmer ground, and began to close the distance. The man, however, was not looking back and continued his path. Kirsten saw him put one foot in, water splashing here and there. As he continued, his feet went down further becoming harder to lift. He inevitably tripped himself up, falling flat on his face. Again, the water gushed out on either side. As he tried to pick himself up, Kirsten arrived, throwing herself into a rugby tackle as the man got back to his feet.

Together, they went down in a large clump, but this time Kirsten was ready. She rolled away, got up to her feet, and as the man stood up, she stepped in towards him, grabbing a wrist and swinging it up behind his back. He cried out loud and swung his other elbow around at her. Kirsten saw it coming, ducked, and then kicked into the man's knees, forcing him to the ground.

'Easy,' said Stewart. 'You take it easy. Who are you and what are you doing here?'

The man swung his elbow again, this time catching Stewart on the side. She drove his arm up harder behind his back and the man cried out. Reaching around behind her, she took out her handcuffs, slapped them on the first wrist before then reaching to the man's second elbow and pulling the other arm around, and snapping the cuffs on the remaining wrist.

'I said easy. You're not going anywhere. There's no way you're getting out of here.' The man's coat was sodden, and part of his face was covered with moss and soil. He'd been wearing a black hat that was now lying somewhere on the moor. Stewart smiled to herself at having finally caught a man who'd escaped her twice.

'Why are you following me? Why were you following me and how are you here? What's your part in all this? I've got you now. You know we'll take you in. I'm in the pursuit of a murderer, but something about you tells me you're not a murderer. You're here for other reasons. What is it?'

'I'm just doing my job.'

'And I'm just doing mine,' said Kirsten. 'I'm a police officer. What do you do?'

'I'm a private investigator.'

'Listed then, are you? We'll find your records somewhere?'

'Not that sort. My client needs demand total confidentiality.'

'Well, that's great because you can remain totally confident that I'll put you in jail, and you'll start to get tied into the murders we're investigating.'

'You said murderer before. Murders now. What murders?' asked the man. 'I'm not looking into any murders. Nobody's been murdered.'

'There's two dead on an oil rig. I've got another one dead in the Cairngorms,' said Stewart. 'What do you mean? No murders.'

'I'm looking for the thieves. I'm looking for who took the art. My client had art stolen and I'm looking for the thieves.'

'Who's your client?' asked Stewart. But the man said nothing. 'I ask again,' said Stewart. 'Who is your client?'

'I said that my client demands a level of confidentiality. I'm not looking for the murderer. I've not been involved in any murders. I am looking for artwork for my client. Something he owned that has been stolen.'

'Oh, if something has been stolen, why don't they go to the police? Why isn't he talking to us?'

'Because what was stolen from him was obtained in an illegal fashion.'

'Who is he?'

'I don't get my work by talking about my clients like that. That's all you're getting from me. You asked why I'm here. That's why I'm here. I'm trying to find his property.'

'Well, you're going to sit inside a cell until my boss gets here,' said Stewart. 'Now up!' She held the man up by the wrist and he rose, not wanting his arms to be driven further up his back. Together they marched across the moor and as they entered the small gate at the back of James Macleod's house, she saw the man standing in his dressing gown.

'Mr Macleod. DC Stewart. I'm just taking this man down the station. Says he's looking for some artwork I think you know about.'

Kirsten can see the look in James Macleod's eyes, the fear, but the voice said nothing.

'Very good then. I think you should come down to the station with me as well. Go get changed, please.'

Chapter 19

Macleod had never thought he would get used to landing at Stornoway Airport. So often, there was a heavy wind or the plane might come in crabbing to one side before swinging around quickly, and landing in a straight line. The Saab 340s were also noisy. Macleod was not a good flier to begin with, but this time he was smiling. Stewart had brought in the goods, and the man was now sitting in a cell down at Stornoway Police Station. Now on his way to interview him, Macleod felt the investigation may finally be going somewhere. Finally, he might actually get an understanding of what was going on.

Ross had reported good news as well. It seemed that there might have been a theft involved, and Macleod was starting to form a picture of a team who could commit a robbery. His problem was making that team up. Why was this group of loose men and a woman so keen to do a robbery of this sort? How did they have a contact into the underworld? That's a side of the art black market that even he didn't know well. The man Stewart had captured clearly did, or he was learning about it very quickly.

The sun was shining as Macleod entered Stornoway Police

Station and shook hands with the Duty Sergeant. He had been there several times and while he didn't know everyone by name, he certainly had a familiarity with the faces. Hope had a bounce in her step as well. He could feel his team suddenly engaging much more in the case, now they had their teeth into something. So far, they'd been swimming around in the dark. That was not unusual. Now, just maybe, they were getting a proper understanding.

When Macleod entered the interview room, he saw a man in black shirt and trousers who looked incredibly calm. Stewart had told him the man had said nothing. Macleod asked Hope to remain outside, instead taking Stewart in with him. As a matter of familiarity, sometimes when put under pressure, people would turn to those they knew. Although Stewart was still obviously the person who had brought the man in, he did at least know her more than Macleod, and a female face was always good with a man. It was a built-in reaction, the idea of the gentler sex, those who would be more likely to be compassionate towards you. Macleod thought about Hope and Stewart; they certainly didn't live up to that billing. They would be as ruthless in the case as he would. In fact, Ross was probably the one you really wanted to be there in your corner. If he had not been in with a suspect, Macleod might have smirked.

Macleod sat down, while Stewart made sure that the correct recording equipment was on and detailed the situation for the tape.

'Now then, you've been following our constable around, physically abusing the people she's been talking to in order to obtain information. You also were captured running away from a suspect in a murder inquiry from whom you were trying to force information before being brought down by my constable here. She reported that you said you were a private eye, but you're not registered or at least I don't think you're registered, because you haven't given us a name yet. You also won't tell us who your client is. Let's start at the beginning. Who are you?'

The man was silent. He stared straight at Macleod, his face not wavering. They had cleaned off the mud from the side of the face, but there still remained an occasional fleck of dirt. Macleod could hold a stare as much as anyone, but this sort of impassive response was not going to help him get any further.

'Okay. You can be like that, but I tell you right now, I'm running your face through our computers. You've been about and you've been doing things. I'll know who you are. You said it was something to do with artwork. Let's get onto our team, the ones that look after that side of things. I bet they'll know you in five minutes.' Macleod turned and waved to an invisible window behind him where Hope was looking in. She entered the room and Macleod whispered to her to give Clarissa a call, show the man's picture. The small group then sat in silence, awaiting the return of Hope. She was back five minutes later and placed a sheet in front of Macleod that had the man's face on it and a large amount of detail of who he was and what he was doing.

'Martin Gopher. Well, that's a made-up name, if I've ever heard of one. I may not know who you are really, but you go by the name of Martin Gopher. Well, Martin, I've got enough here to hold you forever. Our arts team are actually looking for you. There's a couple of cases here with GBH. I'm looking at them and I think they're fairly watertight. You could be going away for a stretch.'

'You won't get the name of my client. If it's a stretch, it's a stretch. That's the business. You don't get caught. I got caught so I'll do my time. You won't get the name of my client.'

'No, but you may not have to do time. You see, I'm not after your client. I'm after a murderer who killed three people. What I want to know, Martin, is what you're doing, who you're looking for, and why you're looking for them, because I think the story you tell me is going to enable me to work out who killed who. If you can do that for me, then we may not have to go full tilt here about these GBH charges.'

The man stared at Macleod, and then he looked over at Stewart. That was it for Macleod. He's buckling. He doesn't like the idea of a stretch, but he knows he doesn't have to give up his client to get out of it. He's looking at Stewart to see if it's going to be for real. Then Macleod saw the customary push of the glasses back up the nose. *Good, Kirsten. Good. He's not getting help from you. He's going to come back to me.'*

'Okay. If I say what I'm doing, you can get me off these charges?'

'Maybe off's a bit much, reduced sentence, maybe you won't serve time at all. I think that's more likely.'

The man looked at Macleod, 'Well, that'll have to do. Can I get that in writing?'

Macleod looked at him. 'Seriously, how long have you been an operator? You want it in writing? I can't put that sort of thing in writing. By the way, you haven't given me anything yet.'

'My boss, the client, the one I'm working for, had a number of artworks, a collection that he obtained by his own methods. Nothing to do with me. He kept them in a private collection, and then they were stolen one night. I know he wouldn't come to you about that, because, well, he shouldn't have had them in the first place, but he needed to get them back. I started doing a little bit of spade work around that. Let's just say that James Macleod got my attention. In fact, not just him, but a crowd from Stornoway got my attention. It started with Gemma Nicholson. She's quite a shaker, moves about in the art world circles. She can get you what you want. I take it you know the house she lives in.'

'Why would you think I would know her house?' asked Macleod.

'Well, I thought you're on the same thing as me. No?'

'I don't know yet,' said Macleod, 'that's what I'm trying to find out. Continue.'

'Gemma Nicholson, she works on the side. You see her at all the auctions moving about, but you really notice her at the auctions of people selling the big stuff up. Stuff you really want if you're a collector, things people with real money have. Then when they don't get it, she'll approach people sometimes. Ask them if they want it. She's done that more than once. She's well-known for it. Nothing proved, of course. Maybe not well-known to your people or maybe she is. Maybe she's just darn good covering her tracks, but her team got caught previously. Not her, but the crew she'd used. Word was, she was training up a new crew. One that was hungry for money.

'Don't get me wrong; this isn't an overnight thing. This would've happened over eighteen months to two years. When I started investigating into it, I realized that her husband was involved. I started tracing connections of his. It turned out that there was a number of Macleods up here as well as her sister-in-law that may have been involved. See, they've all got skills. Electricians, cleaning. People able to shift stuff about.

One of them was strong, very strong. Alastair Nicholson, her husband, built like a brick house. DJ Macleod, he can do electrics. Ian Macleod, let's say he's good at taking care of things. He understands how to treat things gently. When you break into somewhere, like my boss', you need to know how to put things back. Delicate hand that man. James Macleod, again, understanding of electrics, understanding of systems. Then there was Angus Macleod, younger guy, good buddy of Alastair Nicholson's apparently back here in the day. They say he can drive a car extremely well.

'Are you sure they're all a team?' asked Macleod.

'Definitely.'

'You didn't mention Mairi Nicholson,' said Macleod.

'No, I didn't, but I reckon she's your leader. She's the one that talked him into it. You see, the thing about Alastair Nicholson was from what I gather, he's not much of a leader. Gentle, even if he is built like a brick house. Mairi Nicholson, she's something else.'

'You're interesting me now,' said Macleod, 'because two of the people you've mentioned are dead.'

'Dead? It wasn't me, and it wasn't my boss either. We don't do that sort of thing. In truth, he might've made sure that he couldn't lift up a cup again. Given him something to remember him by, but he rarely kills someone. The problem with that is dead people don't talk. People who have been through life-changing situations, people who are now unable to walk, things like that, sometimes they carry much more weight. You can also lean on them to do other things. Not me, of course. I just investigate. I don't carry any of that side of things out.'

'Of course, you don't,' said Macleod; 'wouldn't dream of it, but there's another man dead. A Mr Carmichael. Ever heard

163

of him?'

'No, I haven't, but there was somebody else. There was somebody else who ran the goods. You see, I'm convinced that those who did it got out of the area very, very quickly, but the goods went elsewhere. We tried to track down those that had done it. I came over here to Stornoway as soon as I realized that was Nicholson's crew, I was checking out Alastair Nicholson's contacts, but of course, nobody was here. They all seemed to have disappeared.'

'It's because they were on an oil rig,' said Macleod. 'All of them on an oil rig. What else do you know?'

'I don't,' said the man. 'That's where I'm at. I came over here and I'm checking around things, and of course, your officer's here going into similar places, asking questions. She dropped into Angus Macleod's house, saw her talking to the neighbour. Then she went to the Model Aircraft Club, then she chased me. I thought she must be onto something. I followed her down to the bar, saw her talking to that girl. I was trying to see what she was finding out. Then I realized, when I was doing reconnaissance on the houses, James Macleod was back. It's why I went to see him, and then she pops up. Quite a find, Inspector, knows how to handle herself.'

'All my officers can handle themselves. Don't forget that. Have you got anything more for me?'

'No,' said the man. 'That's it. That enough for you?'

'Well, we'll have to see.'

'It'll be enough so this GBH charge doesn't stick?'

'If I'm honest with you,' said Macleod, 'I'm not sure it would've stuck anyway. Thank you for your help.' Macleod could see the thunder in the man's face. 'Don't be like that,' said Macleod. 'I could do you with assaulting that girl; I could do you with assaulting James Macleod. I won't, and I'm going to let you walk out of here as if nothing's happened, so your boss doesn't know. So he doesn't come around and break your fingers and your legs. That's my deal with you. If you're not happy with that, we can stay here a lot longer. I reckon he'd kill you believing you're talking.'

The man shook his head and then stared at Kirsten. 'You should learn from him. Think about the old ones. The old coppers, right bastards.'

'Thank you for your time, Mr Gopher. You're free to go at this time. Hopefully, I won't have further need for you, and if you stay away from this case from now on, I probably won't. I see your face about, you'll be back in here with me. Do we understand each other, sir?'

The man nodded, sitting back, resigned, in his chair.

Macleod called for the Duty Sergeant and left the room, making his way back to a small office the Stornoway Police had given them. Once he'd gathered his obligatory cup of coffee, Macleod stayed in a small circle with Hope and Stewart.

'What do you make of it, boss?' asked Stewart. 'I mean, it seems that the group were involved. It seems that they did this robbery, but where's the goods?'

'He said the goods went elsewhere. They needed somebody else. My money's on Carmichael. Mairi Nicholson needed somebody she could trust, somebody she had something on. All that nonsense in the past, the relationship, et cetera. Carmichael's moved on from that. She could bring that all back up. We need to look at him. We need to get Ross onto that. I believe that's where we go next. Up here, we need to keep an eye on these guys. We haven't got anything yet, so let's observe them. Let them move about. See if they go near each other. See if we can find anything.'

'But what about the murder?' said Hope. 'Where does the murder come in to it?'

'I don't know,' said Macleod. 'We need to get inside the dynamic of the group. We need to start understanding them. How they operated with each other. Gemma Nicholson was the way in, but from what he said, Mairi Nicholson ran the group. Gemma Nicholson was the contact into the art world, but it sounds like she used different people to obtain the artworks for the clients. I don't think she got her hands dirty. There must've been somebody needing the money. These guys weren't involved in it before. Suddenly, they're onto it. I wonder what sort of money was involved,' said Macleod.

'Life-changing then,' said Hope. 'If your life could change you'd do it, wouldn't you?

Macleod started. 'What? What do mean "You'd do it?"'

'Not me, or Stewart. Them. They've got a monotonous life. Maybe that's not what they want. Maybe that's the catch. Maybe being Gemma's guy meant that Alastair had to do it. Had to do it for his wife. Something's taking them from being a bunch of people to being a bunch of criminals and breaking into somewhere. How do they do it?'

'We find the mystery about them, we'll solve who did the murders,' said Macleod. 'It's time we got to know these people an awful lot better.'

Chapter 20

Ross felt the hair, as little as there was of it on his head, being blown back with the spring sunshine pouring down on him. Sitting in the open-top car Clarissa had brought with her, he found himself quite taken by the woman, older than him and clearly quite eccentric. She had been delighted when he called up again, asking for further assistance. Meeting up at a car park just outside Inverness, she insisted on taking her car, which no longer was a Jaguar. Instead, a small green open-top car, possibly a classic restoration from the '60s. Ross didn't know. Not that he cared either as he stretched out on the leather seat and let the glory of the Highlands encompass him, leaving the monotony of negotiating the road to Clarissa.

Today, she looked radiant even to Ross who had absolutely no interest in her from a sexual point of view, but instead, would have described her as glorious for simply her character. The woman had cried, 'Hop in, Mr Ross,' as she pulled the car up beside him, never stopping the engine before tearing away off to the A9. The pair were heading for Pitlochry, that outpost between Perth and Inverness, a thriving community, and somewhere many tourists saw as the hub of the lower part of the Highlands. As they drove through the mountains, Ross looked at the glorious greens and brown hues and the occasional loch shining under the sun. It wasn't warm, rather a more pleasant temperature, one you can happily walk about in and maybe even cool enough for a small jumper. Clarissa herself was wearing a large pair of shades with a thin-strapped pale blue top with matching culottes. Everything about her exuded fun and excitement, and Ross was more than happy to be caught up in the vibe. It certainly made a change from Macleod.

The reason for calling in Clarissa was to see if she could help track down the missing artwork. Ross knew that she had identified which pictures were missing, so he was asking for her expertise in the field to find a likely fence for the items. Given that Carmichael had been found dead in the Cairngorms, it seemed obvious that either Inverness or anywhere south could have been used to find a fence, someone to shift on the artwork, but Clarissa had instantly told him they were heading for Pitlochry. In fact, she said she had been planning to go that way herself, having realized what pictures were missing.

As they drove through Pitlochry, marrying the quaint style with the many trees and houses packed away inside the small parts of forest, Ross realized he was becoming very much a backseat passenger. It was his investigation or at least his team's, but Clarissa acted as if he was merely a tourist along for the ride, and she pointed out interesting landmarks and points of history all the way from Inverness down to Pitlochry. Many of them Ross knew because he was no philistine, but on the other hand, the sheer depth of the woman's knowledge was impressive.

'Where exactly are we going?' said Ross, as they drove

through the town and out the far side of it.

'You'll see in a moment; it's a small— looks like a hut, but that's just a cover. She sells artwork, quite new on the scene as well. Father was in the same line of work. Good job I've got you with me as well as she's turned many a man's head. I've got the feeling you won't be.' Ross cast a glance at Clarissa. Then they both laughed together. 'I hope you don't mind,' she said. 'Quite obvious, and you may have mentioned it.'

'You should tell my boss then,' said Ross. 'It took him a while to catch on.'

'Probably took a blunt statement,' said Clarissa, and again began to laugh heartily, 'But just be careful. I don't want to spook this girl either.'

Clarissa pulled up to a small farmhouse just beyond the edge of Pitlochry. The door opened and a young woman of maybe no more than twenty-five emerged dressed in jeans, Wellington boots, and a rather plain t-shirt that had dirty streaks around it. The jeans were filthy and the boots seemed to be covered in some sort of caked mud or possibly animal excrement.

'Hi,' said the girl. 'If you're looking for the artwork, it's round the back in the shed. I can be with you in five minutes. Just been feeding the chickens.'

'Delightful,' shouted Clarissa. 'You happy if we just go on in?'

'Of course, just make a note of anything you like. I can tell you more about it when I'm in. As I said, five minutes.'

Clarissa spun the wheel of the car, flagging up a load of dust as she made her way along a track to the rear of the farmhouse.

It was indeed a large barn, two-story, by the look of it. A rather pale drab white on the outside with a rather modern sign saying, *Julie Anscombe, Dealer in Art and Photographic Wares.*

'Look at the sign,' said Clarissa. 'How crass and yet brilliant. You have to hand it to her.'

Ross was slightly bemused. He had no idea what sort of sign you should put up as a genuine purveyor in expensive art, but he nodded politely, hanging on to his seat as Clarissa threw the car about before coming to a sharp halt outside the front door. As she leapt out and made her way round the front of the car towards the shed, Ross noticed the knee-length boots she was wearing. There were minimal heels on them and they were quite a change from the high stilettos she had worn the previous time they'd met.

'Ah, yes, the boots, easier to run in. This girl might run so let's be careful,' said Clarissa. 'Let's go in and see what a crock of crap tourists will buy these days.'

Ross was amused by the woman. She had such a way of speaking, and then suddenly she would throw in the odd crass comment. Maybe that was what the upper class did. Ross did not know— he'd been brought up on an estate.

'Right, darling, let's have a look.' Clarissa pushed open the door which creaked. Inside, the barn was well lit up, not just with electric light, but due to several large windows that cascaded light in a warm glow.

'You can see she knows how to light the place. But let's see what you think first. On the far wall, what do you think of that?' said Clarissa striding her way towards a piece of art on the wall that was at least the size of a man.

'It's got to be expensive,' said Ross, 'hasn't it? Look at the size of it.'

'What do you think of the painting?' said Clarissa. 'The style, the way it's done. What does it make you feel?' Ross looked up at the woman in the picture. She had flowing ringlets of hair dropping down onto bare shoulders. A wispy veil was across her chest. As you made your way down the picture, her legs were suddenly revealed.

'Doesn't really make me feel anything.'

'Not talking about that way,' said Clarissa. 'What does it evoke? Look at it. What do you think? Is it tugging at your heartstrings?'

'No,' said Ross and stepped forward closer to see a dangling tag. He took one look at the price and almost swore. 'Certainly attacks the bank account.'

Clarissa laughed. 'Absolutely, utter crap for the tourists,' she said. 'Look at it, it's terrible. Who on earth painted that?' She took a look at the corner where the artist had signed their name. 'Yes, Alderson; the man was useless.'

'Not to your taste then?' said Julie Anscombe entering the building. The woman had done an amazingly quick turnaround. She was in bare feet with a pair of black slacks on and a white blouse. 'Apologies for the feet,' she said. 'It's just that I wore the Wellies across where a few of the animals escaped yesterday. Left a lot of stuff lying around but please feel free to browse, see what you like. I can tell you about any of the pictures if you wish.'

'Let's be honest, dear. This man with me is a commercial banker. He's not interested in the style that you've got here. He's interested in what he can acquire, what he can put cash into, something that will hold its value properly. I'm here to verify it for him. I know this is the tourist shop. We want to see the proper stuff.'

'Who told you I did proper artwork?'

'Recently saw a collection, dropped your name. His Highness

Philippe said it to me, said you're able to assist Phil at spotting his collection. Wouldn't tell me what with though; said it was exquisite.'

'Well, of course,' she said. 'He said someone would be coming. Let's take a look up top.'

With that, the woman pressed a button on the wall and the ceiling above Ross began to descend. Slowly, a pair of steps came down to touch the ground.

'That's handy,' said Ross. 'Nice piece of engineering as well.'

'What did I tell you?' laughed Clarissa. 'Commercial banker, more interested in nuts and bolts. Shall we?'

'By all means,' said Julie. 'I'll close it up once we're up top; keep the tourists out.'

They made their way up the wooden steps that had descended from above and found themselves on a replica of the room below. There was plenty of light and many pictures hanging on the wall, but this time, Ross decided they must have been looking at higher quality material for Clarissa was almost licking her lips. 'Delightful, dear,' she said. 'Absolutely delightful. Just give me a few minutes to see what would suit this gentleman.'

'By all means, take your time. I'm sure you'll be able to find what you're looking for.'

Ross tagged along behind Clarissa, studying each picture as she went along. When she reached the end of one wall, Ross shook his shoulders. 'Are any of these any good?' he said. Clarissa turned in a low whisper and said, 'They're all exceptionally good. They're all actual paintings, and we could buy any of these for anything from £5,000 to £10,000. They're very neat. Some of them haven't even been pinched. This is some genuine trading she does as well. It's not what we're looking for though.'

'What are we looking for then?'

'I'll tell you when I see it.' With that, Clarissa turned on her heel, marched across the back wall, staring at the pictures for a while. It took her twenty minutes to go round the entire collection but Julie Anscombe showed no impatience. When she'd finished, Clarissa walked over to the woman and proffered her hand. 'Can I congratulate you on a magnificent collection, but I want those three over there.'

'The Shamir's, excellent choice. Not many Norwegian artists in here.'

'He is rather good, and like I say, my friend has money to put away. They should easily cover £20,000 to £30,000. I'll have Philippe send the money over.'

Julie Anscombe shook her hand. 'Much appreciated,' she said. 'I'll just get them sorted for you.'

With that, the woman went over to the pictures, took them down off the wall, and began to wrap them up. Ross leaned over Clarissa's shoulder. 'Well, now we've got them. Do we move?' Clarissa waved a hand at him and then gave him a stare that told him to keep quiet. When Julie Anscombe had finished her wrapping, she carried the pictures out to the car for Clarissa, delicately putting them into the boot.

'Love the car as well,' said Julie. 'Heard a lot about you, much appreciated. Tell Philippe, any time he needs something else, just to drop me a line.'

'I will indeed, absolutely,' said Clarissa. 'Might even drop by myself sometime. There's a few of the other things up there that take my fancy.'

'Really?'

'Really. The Austin for one, lovely, would look great out the back of my house. It needs a bit of sunlight around it though, don't you think?'

'I can see you know what you're on about,' said Julie. 'It's good to deal with somebody that appreciates the art and not just the money behind it.'

'I so know what you mean,' said Clarissa, starting up the car and then waving extravagantly as she drove off.

Ross was bemused. They had come along, managed to get up to the better pictures, then bought a couple without handing over any money and had simply driven away. 'So, what do we do now?' asked Ross.

'In a minute, dear,' said Clarissa and continued to drive out into the country. After a while, she pulled into a layby. Carefully, she opened her boot and took out a small knife. Ross watched as she delicately unveiled one of the packages and set the picture on the rear seat of the car.

'What do you see, constable?'

'Well, it's a picture, isn't it?'

'Well, I can see why Macleod keeps you on his team. Look closer.'

Ross looked closer. He couldn't see anything other than a picture of a rather quaint house with a sunrise behind it.

'Yes. I see I'm going to have to work on you. Utter rubbish. See the brushstrokes in the top corner? They're not right. It's a copy. Not a great copy but I've seen worse.'

'So why have we got a copy? Are you telling me she didn't have the pictures after all?'

Delicately, Clarissa cut around the edge of the frame and then removed the cloth the picture was painted on. Behind it, Ross saw another picture. 'Wow,' he said. 'Are these the ones we're after?' and reached forward.

Clarissa grabbed his hand. 'Don't. Don't touch it. I just needed confirmation.' Delicately, she put the picture to one side. She then performed the same operation on the other two pictures, each time finding a picture inside that was related closely to the one she'd uncovered. 'We need to get these somewhere and we need to get someone to come and arrest that young woman,' said Clarissa.

'Well, throw them in the boot and we'll drive back and arrest her now,' said Ross.

'Throw them in the boot? I don't know what you do on the murder team, but with evidence as expensive as that, we certainly don't muck about.'

'Wow,' said Ross, 'what are we looking at then? What £20,000, £30,000, £40,000?'

'You won't get change of £10 million on that,' said Clarissa and watched Ross's face. 'As I said, dear, we need to get these somewhere safe and someone out to arrest that young woman.'

Chapter 21

Macleod stood impatiently as Hope made the connect call through and linked her laptop up so that Macleod would be able to see Ross and the art detective on the screen of the computer. He was never good at these sorts of things. He left it up to the others in the team to set them up for him. He could do it but it would take several minutes more and everybody would just get frustrated.

In the meantime, Macleod was thinking exactly how he was going to work out what was going on within the group. At some point, they would make a move for their money. At some point, they would have to get away with what they'd done. Right now, he did not know where that would be or when it would be. He had left Ross with his new fine art colleague to discover where the goods had been shipped to. In truth, he was out of his field, as was Ross. Certainly, the female detective they brought in from the other department had come up trumps and without her, the investigation would not have moved forward. They would have been sitting blind, ducks hoping they could follow the river on sound alone without seeing what was going on.

'It's ready, sir. I think Ross is there.'

'Hello, Hope, can you hear me?' Ross's face emerged loomed large on the screen.

'Yes, I've got you, Alan,' said Hope. 'It's loud and clear. The inspector's right here.' Hope stepped back from the screen and indicated Macleod should sit down. He plonked himself on the chair, gave a moment's thought to how he would look on the screen given that there was a third party here, and made a slight adjustment on his tie.

'What's the news, Ross?'

'Big, sir. We found the goods and we've made an arrest.'

'Arrest?' said Macleod in surprise. 'Already?'

'Yes, sir. Sergeant Urquhart here was able to trace the fence. When we got there, we were able to ascertain where the goods were and she uncovered them. In fairness, that's a very brief summary. They were hidden behind some other paintings. I wouldn't have had a clue what was going on but the sergeant was right on the money. Apparently, they've been tracking the movement of these paintings for a while. The items getting stolen threw a bit of a spanner in the works in terms of their investigation but they've been recovered and they've brought in a fence as well. Hopefully, they're going to be able to link it back to whoever was at the top of the chain.'

'Well done, Ross. Excellent and well done to your colleague. I'm afraid she's not on the screen.'

Ross stood up and with a polite hand indicated to someone off-screen that they should sit down. Macleod was rather taken aback as a woman with a scarf around her neck and an elegant tight-fitting blouse, sat down before him. He was waiting for her to remove the pair of sunglasses on her face, but she didn't do so.

'Inspector Macleod,' she said. 'Damn fine to meet you. I'm

177

pleased to record Constable Ross, whilst being an abject failure in the subject of art, was an admirable sparring partner. I'm sure we could turn him into a commercial banker any day.'

Macleod was rather taken aback. Most officers that spoke to him had an air of reverence and almost fear at times. He was well known throughout the force and especially now in the Inverness area, having been resident here for a while. Everyone knew the tough times he'd faced having been targeted himself by certain perpetrators and also about how dogged he was and what he expected from people.

'Well, that's rather nice to say, Sergeant Urquhart.'

'Really, Inspector. That's all rather formal. It's Clarissa. I believe we have to address each other this way now anyway. Don't we? We've done a rather spiffing job today. It's turned out rather splendidly, and I have to say, the only downside is, it's probably blown my cover. I've been working on that for several years now, but now the bus has come in, and we're going to have to start busting back up the line. These blighters are going to know who I am, so it looks like I'm back behind the desk and doing a little bit less of the reconnaissance work for a while. Ho-hum, we shall see, but Ross here says that this will help you with your murder investigation.'

'Right,' said Macleod, a little taken aback. 'If you could just fill me in on exactly what happened in terms of the goods and possibly what happened with my group here in Stornoway, I'd be rather pleased to know. At the moment, we're no further forward with identifying who the murderer was.'

'But, of course, Inspector. Basically, Lord Argyle— not directly, but certain of his contacts— stole a few rather expensive paintings. When I say expensive, I'm talking in the tens of millions. He does not put these on display, obviously. It is kept in the very private collection, but we've been watching Gemma Nicholson, the wife of Alastair Nicholson, for some time. She's quite a mover. They have a rather expensive house, which I believe your good man here, Ross, was nearly burnt alive in, and it seems that she organized an attempt to steal the paintings. She hauled a team together, I think, through her husband, Alastair who worked out on the rig. It looks like they were pulling people from different walks of life and training them up. May have taken quite a while. The thing about these paintings is they've been missing for a while as well. Lord Argyle's moved them several times because he has several estates. Gemma somehow has worked out where they were and decided to take them. If you can move these on, it's a game-changer in somebody's life. Before, Gemma was small fry but whatever she did, she learnt about this and she's gone for it big time.'

'So, where's the money from this?' asked Macleod. 'Where do the proceeds come in?'

'It'll have been paid on already. I believe the fence, that is the woman we picked up today, Julie Anscombe, has already been paid, or rather, she's passed a payment on from those that she contacted. It's a person outside of this country but the money we've looked at and from the information that Julie's told us, seems to have been routed through a Swiss bank account. It was then transferred and taken out. From what we can gather, and these investigations are quite preliminary, the money may have been brought to the Isle of Lewis and hidden.'

'Hidden? In what way?'

'You need to check the yachts that have come in recently. Look out for these ones and you'll not miss them. Shalimar, Hoppy Grandeur, Bay of Plenty. Contact Stornoway coastguard, see if any of them have been in the locality. If they have, the money has been dropped. You'll not be able to pull in any of the boats; there'll be gone by now and secondly, there won't be anything on board, nothing to trace them. They're owned by the man who has bought these paintings. We can't touch him. It's very awkward, but we can cut off the source which is what we've done.

'We've retrieved the paintings and he's going to be damn furious. Your guys might get wind of this. If they do, I would suspect they would run because he'll come looking for his paintings. After all, they've got his money. The fence was expecting someone to come and from a tip-off we had, the fence was told that whoever was coming would understand which paintings were which. I didn't know what this meant, but when I got upstairs inside the gallery, the private one that she had, three portraits were fakes. It had to be them. The original paintings were hiding behind the fakes. You drop the right name and suddenly you're there. Of course, our fence only knew it was going to be a pickup. Julie Anscombe has acted exactly as been asked. It's just we intercepted it. So, it's over to you, Inspector. I don't know how that helps your murder inquiry, but what I can tell you is that money is probably on Lewis and they'll make a move for it soon.'

'Right,' said Macleod, trying to digest all the information. 'We best get cracking. Thank you kindly, Clarissa.'

'Always a pleasure inspector. Anytime you need me, just give a call and by all means, send this delightful young man, my way. By the way, you're not as gruff as they say you are.'

Macleod sat back in his chair unable to speak. What should he say to this woman? Normally in his conversations with police colleagues, he led the line of inquiry. He said where the conversation was going but she had taken it on board and run with it. Looking at her, she did not strike him as a sergeant, and he was wondering what the story was behind her role. Still, she had done him a favour, so Macleod simply smiled and said thank you.

After confirming with Ross that he should start to make his way over to Stornoway whenever possible, Macleod took the rest of his small team through into the room allocated to them by Stornoway police.

'Do we lift them, sir?' asked Hope.

'Lift them and do what?' asked Macleod. 'I can't charge anybody. We can't prove that they actually stole the paintings. The only link that is going to come through there now is if Gemma Nicholson squeals on them. If we catch them picking up the money, we've got them.'

'How do we nail them for the murder then?' asked Stewart.

'I'm not sure we can; without Gemma Nicholson, we might be scuppered on that. Somebody had to bring Carmichael in. Now, if Nicholson squeals, we're okay but we got a problem at the moment. Where is she? She hasn't come back to her house yet and if I'm right, the reason for that is because Lord Argyle was onto her.'

'Maybe she saw Ross was in the shed and she set fire to it,' suggested Stewart. 'She saw him with the camera, saw him looking and taking photographs of the very theft they had committed. Maybe that's why she tried to bump him off so she thinks that we're after her, not Argyle.'

'Then, she'd run,' said Hope. 'That makes much more sense. Much more sense that she'd run, Seoras; we need to get an all-persons-out on her, ports everywhere, see if they can stop her before she leaves the country.'

'Get on it, Hope.'

As Hope left the room, Stewart turned back to her Inspector. 'Sir— sorry, Seoras— how do we catch them, boss? Are we just sitting around waiting for them to make a move?'

'We have to. We'll keep tabs on the boys, also Mairi Nicholson if we can find her. She hasn't shown up yet anywhere.'

'According to the flight logs though, she didn't arrive, despite being booked on a flight here,' said Stewart, 'but I never saw her arrive. A couple of the constables have confirmed that DJ's been here as has Ian and James, although they've not contacted each other as far as we know. I've got a couple of constables just keeping an eye on them at this time. We just sit and wait for them to move?'

'There's nothing else we can do, Stewart, what else have we got? We know where these three are. Mairi Nicholson, we don't. Gemma Nicholson, we don't either. They're the smart ones. The other guys, they're obviously waiting for instruction so we bide our time. In the meantime, I haven't eaten. I'm going to go and grab something to eat. While I'm doing that, I'm going to make a phone call. I need to talk to someone who knew them back then, someone who knew what they were like together.'

'Sir?'

'The problem we've got is that nowadays, they say they haven't seen each other. We don't have them congregating anywhere. Everyone is apart. Heck, Alastair was on the mainland, not even here in Lewis. I need to go back to what the relationships were, back to understand it, because Carmichael's involved as well. It's like the old team again, back at that scandal. If I can do that, I'll understand what's going on.' Macleod stood up and left the room, aware of the verbal musings of Stewart. She was churning over his words and a wry smile came across his face. That's why she was on the team, to check his thinking, to check his logic. She was good at that.

The small kitchenette in Stornoway Police Station was able to afford a microwaved meal to Macleod. As he sat down looking at the shepherd's pie, he groaned. If he had been at home, Jane would have been making something decent. Something more than acceptable. Macleod smiled; hopefully, he would be home soon.

The door to the kitchen burst open and Hope ran in.

'Sir, one of them is moving, DJ. Apparently, he got a phone call and then tore out of the house. He's on his way to somewhere.'

'Well, you've got it, Hope. Take Stewart, bring him in.'

'Sir, are you sure? You don't want to come with us? Be there. See what they're doing?'

'No,' said Macleod. 'You and Stewart can take this one. Pick him up, bring him in. Hang on a minute to see if you can find the money, okay? See where they are going to be with it. Stewart knows this lot from before. You're more than capable of running this, Hope. Pick them up.'

McGrath stared at him. 'What are you up to?'

'I'm not up to anything, Hope. I'm just going to tie up the loose ends. You sort the money. I'll sort the murder.'

Chapter 22

Macleod stood outside the school he remembered from his youth. Of course, things have changed since he was here. It still was in essence the same building; parts had been built, others demolished. Of course, they had. But a part of his life had been spent here. Now coming back, he thought he would feel almost nostalgic. It was a time before he had met his wife, back when he'd been brought up in the strict religious home life that his mother and father had imposed.

Part of him was grateful for it, although he was still trying to reconcile the way the church had treated his wife after they got married. Certainly, there was no room for frivolity, no room for a free spirit. Back in the day at school, the same was true. It had not bothered Seoras. He had complied. He had gotten on and he had done well. When he joined the police force, his mother said the school had played such a large part to in it, but now, he just needed information from a different era in this building.

As he stood in the car park, there was no one around. It was Saturday, the school was shut, and it was late evening. Although the nights were now lighter until about nine o'clock, it was starting to dim, the chill of the air becoming more apparent. The day had been a decent one. No rain, not that much cloud. The temperatures had soared to almost double figures for April. It was surprisingly good. Macleod heard a voice shouting at him from behind.

'My apologies, Inspector. I'm slightly late. How are you?'

Macleod turned around and saw a face he recognized. Anneline McKinney had served at the school for a long time, some forty years in total. In the middle of that, she had spanned the time during which the scandal had been covered up. The indiscretions of Carmichael, along with Mairi Nicholson and the rest of the troop, had required careful manoeuvering by the school at a time when bringing things to the fore simply didn't happen. Reputations had to be upheld.

'Seoras Macleod. You've done well for yourself. Your mother had always said you'd do well. I read about you. I see you on the news in those cases; mind you, it's worrying you, isn't it? Look at your face. Good to see you, boy, though. Good to see you.'

'Mrs McKinney, it's been so long. How are you?'

'I'm old, Seoras, older than you. Look at me. I can walk. I can talk. What more do you want when you're eighty? I can still live a little. The good Lord has been kind to me. I think He's been good to you as well, especially after what happened.'

This is what Macleod did not want. Nowadays, he was over the death of his wife. Her suicide out by Holm when she'd taken herself into the sea was now a thing of the past and not present company. He was over it. Well, when he said over, as over as you ever got. He was at peace with it. That was more accurate, but only in so much as long as people didn't bring it up.

'I'm sorry to drag you out, Mrs. McKinney. I need to know something that went on here in the school.'

'Oh,' said the woman. 'Forty years, a lot went on in this school. What are you talking about?'

'Something they kept quiet. Mairi Nicholson. Mr Carmichael.' Macleod saw the woman's face redden.

'Why'd you want to drag that up? Just a silly girl and a silly man. I don't know what he saw in her.'

'Is that the real story?'

'Are you accusing me of lying, Seoras Macleod? I'm a woman of God, a good woman. I go Sunday and I go Wednesday to the prayer meeting. I'm a good woman. I'll not lie to you.'

'Just a silly girl and a silly man?' said Seoras. 'That doesn't sound like something to be covered up. It might've been a scandal, but I'm sure there were others doing that. Tell him to stop it. Keep it quiet. She'd have been out of the school in a year or two. Nobody would have cared. This was more than that, wasn't it?'

'That's why you went to the police force. You could always read people. Your mother said that. She said, she'd tell you half of something and you'd ask for the rest of it. Your father, he just said nothing because he knew you'd be into it. You certainly ended up in the right place. Do you want to drag this out though?'

'I'm not looking to bring any charges. I'm not looking to highlight things. There'd be no point. Carmichael's dead.'

The woman almost stumbled backwards. 'Dead? What happened to him?'

'I think he was murdered.' Macleod watched her face. He could almost feel the cold racing through her.

'Who killed him?' asked Mrs. McKinney.

'That's what I'm trying to establish. I want to know what happened.'

'Like I said, silly boy, silly girl.'

'Like you said, I have a nose for this. Don't lie to me, Anneline. School's not going to go anywhere with this. It's not going to get dragged up in that fashion. I just need to serve some justice. Tell me what happened?'

'Come over here and sit down,' said the woman. 'Sit down beside me and I'll tell you of it. You're right. It wasn't a silly girl. It was a very silly man.'

Macleod helped the woman to a bench and as she sat down, he swore he could hear her bones click. She was older than he remembered but then again, she was older than he. She had bustled about the place and understood everything within the school. For every lead that had been in the school, everyone who had sought to run it and run it efficiently, Anneline McKinney had been at their right hand. She knew everyone's business. She would have heard of things on a daily basis and yet she was so pleasant to speak to.

'Mairi Nicholson was a trollop. You need to understand that, Seoras. She was one of those girls, seventeen and she could turn the head of any man. She knew how to use her hair, and she knew how to use the rest of her. She wanted a lifestyle that this island would never support. She saw all the pictures, all the rock and roll, everything. All of that, that's what she wanted. She wanted more, always.

'Well, Carmichael was *more* at the time. He was only twenty-five, new teacher and he had looks. Don't get me wrong, he had *looks*. Well, she set her eyes on him and that was that, but she had a crowd with her. She'd been going with DJ Macleod, Duncan John, and there was Ian and James as well. They called them the Macleod triplets but they weren't related. Well, as much as any of you Macleod's are not related up here.

'Then there was young Angus. Young Angus, and Alastair, five years younger, but they hung around in the crowd, and that clown Carmichael got involved up in the castle grounds. That's eventually where they found him, stoned out with her on top of him, the rest of them lying around, smacked off their heads except for the young lads. That's when it crashed down but they kept it going for months.'

'It seems to me that she got what she wanted though,' said Macleod. 'I don't understand. Was there any angst when it all fell apart?'

'No, she didn't blame him for that,' said Anneline. 'She blamed him for not taking her away, she blamed him for not having the life she wanted. The thing about her you see, and the thing not a lot of people knew, was she had a wild temper. I remember seeing it. She was looking all pretty one day, the days of the short skirts and the blouses. Nothing compared to today's stuff but back in those days, you were a trollop wearing those, but she wore them and flaunted it.

'This dog came up, small thing. Well, started messing with her, didn't it? Jumping around. The next thing, she's got muddy prints all over her. She was at the back of the school, nobody to see. She kicked the living daylights out of that thing. She went through it, Seoras. I only know because I saw the last bits of it. I had to clear it away, buried the poor thing around the back of the science block. Still there probably. Well, they've probably built a few things on top. All it did was put muddy footprints on her, muddy footprints and she wrecked it. She took its life. That was her when the steam got up.'

'What became of her when she had left?' asked Macleod.

She spent a while trying different schemes, trying to make it but she never did. She always wanted the big time. She's that sort of a girl. She told me once, she'd be quite happy if she could marry a millionaire.

'I heard she was offshore though,' said Macleod.

'She's offshore; you are not telling me the truth of it, are you? You know she's offshore. What's she done?'

'You think she might be any good at burglary?'

'She would be good at anything if she put her mind to it, not because she could do it herself. She'd entice the men. She'd get any man to do what she wanted; she would find the right ones.'

'What about that cohort she used to kick about with?'

'Round her little finger, but they're on the rigs as well, aren't they?'

'I couldn't possibly comment, Mrs McKinney, and I certainly couldn't say any more about it, but Alastair is dead, Angus is dead. I'm afraid someone in that group must have done it.'

'Well, you hear me, Seoras, hear me good. If there's anyone that was going to pull that lot together, it's Mairi Nicholson.'

'Have you heard anything else about her lately, though?' asked Macleod. 'I know she's been working on the rig. I don't know anything about her here.'

'Do you know my boy John?'

'I don't think I've ever met him. How is he doing?'

'Very well, down at the harbour. He knew Mairi Nicholson as well. I warned him well of her of course. John was much older than her, but that was the thing about her. She could turn it on for any guy. You see, she tried it on with John before. Was asking about sailing, John said to me; she was wanting to know how to pilot the boat.'

'What did she want a boat for?'

'He said somebody had given her one.'

'How recent is this?'

'In the last couple of years, maybe a year ago, eighteen months. When he asked her about it, said she was ready for a new life. I thought it was just one of those fads she always went through, a bit of the high life. It didn't come with a crew though. I remember John saying that there was no crew with it.'

'Did she get anyone to help her out with that?'

'As far as I recall,' said Mrs. McKinney, 'somebody did. I can't remember his name but my son remembers the boat she got. He'll remember that.'

* * *

Hope sat in the car looking across the moor at the small caravan based alongside the peat bank. She had gotten out a couple of times to attend to the wheel at the back of her car, taking a jack, hitting it. She walked around checking underneath the car then adjusting this and that. Occasionally, she would watch as Stewart drove past in a different car followed by a number of other unmarked police cars. Her mobile phone was on and it was open.

'Have the three of them arrived?' asked Stewart.

'I see DJ Macleod, Ian, and James has just got here. No Mairi Nicholson yet, and not a single person has stopped to help me with this wheel. I thought this was meant to be a friendly island?'

'You're obviously not flashing enough leg,' said Stewart, and laughed. 'Either that or you look like a dangerous woman;

maybe you're scaring them.'

Hope girlishly threw back her red hair. *I'll scare them*, she thought, and laughed. Her mind wandered back to John Allen and his flat in Inverness. She hadn't called him enough, she was sure of that. She had to speak to him more, but then again, if he was still there, still waiting when she got back . . . well, maybe he would work out. She really hoped so.

McGrath stared over at the caravan. It was an old one, maybe enough for two or three people to stay in the bubble end. Once in its life, it might have been white, but now it was a mix of cream and rust. It was not unusual to find a caravan out by the peat banks. In earlier times, during the summer, some of the men might have lived out here using the sheilings. And then there were some caravans and then there was less and less peat cutting. Nowadays, there was nothing like there used to be and the one thing that Macleod never talked about was cutting them. He seemed to have hated them in his day and she knew that his father had made him do it.

Hope saw someone get out of the caravan. It was DJ Macleod taking a step down. Then he turned around, looked back inside the caravan, and shook his head. Ian Macleod stepped out, followed by James, and there seemed to be a heated debate. Several swear words were able to carry on the air to reach Hope at the car. She kept an ear cupped towards them. There was some debate about that bloody woman: Where was she? Then the men seem to get panicked and one by one, they stepped into their cars to begin to drive along the track back to the main road.

'They're on the move,' said Hope; 'looks like it's a bust. I'm going to corner them off. Find out what they've been doing.' With that, she ran back inside her car, driving it quickly to the

191

end of the path. Soon she was facing them, head-on. Either side of the track was a ditch, and there was nowhere for the men to go. When the car was met head-on, and both parties had braked, Hope stepped out, and made her way to the men.

'Hello again. Do you remember me? DS McGrath. Where is Mairi Nicholson?'

'I don't know what you mean. We just came out to the peat bank.'

'To do what? Inspect it? You haven't got any equipment with you. You've got nothing. You met here to distribute the money.'

'What money?'

'From the job. From the paintings you stole.'

'Hell, she knows,' said Ian.

'Shut up,' said DJ.

'Yeah, we know, and Carmichael's dead.'

'Carmichael's what?' said Ian, and the man started to shake. 'That wasn't me. That wasn't me, and it wasn't me with Angus either, or Alastair. It wasn't me. She's done a runner. Bloody hell, DJ, she's run. She'll have taken the bloody money.'

'Like hell, she's taking that money,' said James. 'Like hell.' Behind her, Hope, could hear the other cars arriving.

'I'm afraid it's time-up, gents,' said Hope. 'If you'd like to accompany me down to the station, I think you can give me a full-on, frank confession about what you know.'

'I didn't kill him. I didn't kill any of them. Do you hear me?' said Ian. 'We were just told to keep stum and we'd get our money. God, she killed Angus. She killed Angus.'

'Did you see that?' asked Hope. 'Did you see her kill him?'

'No. I didn't see her kill him, but somebody killed Alastair.'

'You're too late,' said DJ. 'She'll be gone. She'll be bloody gone. That bitch's played me all of her life. She's damn well gone.'

chapter 23

Mairi Nicholson stepped out of the car and ran the short distance down the pontoons. The sailing yacht was there, as impressive as it had always been. Inside, it had a luxury bridge, everything you could want to steer a vessel like this. There was an impressive engine or the large sails that could be erected. With the right sailor on board, this vessel could take you most anywhere. Tonight, it was taking Mairi away from everything. She'd done it and she was free. She saw the latest in a line of men standing, waving at her. It hadn't taken much to bring him on board.

Michael was Albanian and struggling with the authorities for having entered the country illegally. Back home, he had been a sailor. With a little bit of money and a little bit of her own body, he was now hers, ready to take her wherever. Once she got away, and they had made it past the Mediterranean towards the Middle East, then Michael would disappear as well. For now, she'd need to play him along and, in truth, she'd enjoy her time with him. The man was younger than she. He had a body worth enjoying and he was eager to please. Stepping onto the yacht, she threw her arms around and kissed him.

He seemed somewhat nervous so she ran her hands down

his back, tenderly grabbing his backside. She smacked it, told him to get inside while she undid the ropes. He could take the vessel out. The sun was fading and the night closing in. As she undid the ropes, her heart skipped a beat. There was over five million in the hold. Five million. Life could begin. With five million, she could live however she wanted to. No man would own her. No man would disappoint her again because she was in control. A self-made woman, she'd taken charge. If only he hadn't been so stupid, Alastair would have been here with her.

She shook her head, and the long curls flew in the light wind. Making her way inside the yacht, she stood behind Michael. As he steered the vessel out, she rubbed his bottom and took her hand up his back before cuddling up tight to him. He was nervous, incredibly nervous. She was used to him getting excited whenever she was there. Maybe it was emotion. Maybe it was the moment.

'We're free, Michael. This is us. We are free, out of here. All that money to do what we want with. All that money. Do you understand? You and me have got it made. Just keep the yacht going,' she said. 'I'm tired of running around; I had to get all those idiots together. Police should be picking them up now. Not me. I'm going for a shower. I'm going to freshen up and then I'll come to you. We'll get clear, get away out into the ocean. Tonight, I'm going to make you an incredibly happy man.'

Michael smiled but she did not sense the same excitement in him. *He's just nervous*, she thought. *Just nervous.*

The shower on the yacht was impressive, as good as any she had been in her life. Mairi Nicholson let the lather run down her body. Her shoulders were tight, tense. It had been a long haul, several years of planning, several years of Gemma being persuaded. Gemma always said it wasn't possible, that this team from Stornoway couldn't do it, but she'd been good. She'd got the plans, the schematics; she'd done all the groundwork, but then Gemma was used to that. After all, Alastair was nothing, but a kept man, Gemma was the real operator. When Mairi found that out, she'd seen a way in, her way to paradise, her way to the millions she wanted. Gemma would get her share; she was disappearing off with five million as well.

It had always been the plan to dump the boys in it. She'd stuck around with those losers long enough. Even back in her school days, they were just the clowns, just the ones to do her bidding.

Stepping out of the shower, she rubbed herself down with a towel before putting on a dressing gown and standing in front of the mirror. She adjusted the gown so just enough cleavage was showing. Something to get Michael excited, something to keep his focus on getting them out of there, because the man was going to have a long night. There was no way she was piloting the boat out after all she'd done; Michael could do it. She made her way through the cabin, up to the top deck, to the wheelhouse where Michael was looking out. Something was wrong, something wasn't right. She recognized the fishing boat across from her.

'Why are we still in the harbour, Michael? What's wrong? Is there something wrong with the engine?' Michael was quiet, very quiet. 'Michael, what's the matter? Why are we still here? I told you to take us out. We should be well past Holm by now. Michael?'

There was a cough behind her. 'I'm afraid I insisted that Michael keep us here. You see I wanted a word, Mairi Nicholson. I wanted a word about the death of your brother and the death of Angus Macleod.'

Macleod would have told the woman to get dressed but she had simply sat down and right now he could see more thigh and leg than he'd seen in the last year from Jane. That was saying something, but he found nothing attractive about the woman. Yes, she had the looks. Even at the maturing age of thirty-five, she still seemed as sprightly as a twenty-year-old but now, knowing what she'd done, Macleod could never be attracted.

'Five million in the hold,' said Macleod. 'Three boys looking for their money, ready to talk. You're bang to rights, Mairi. I've got you. There's nowhere to go. I can lift you for the theft; I can put you away for a long time. I can take away the money.

'Michael here will tell me everything. If he's lucky I can get him shipped back to Albania, tap on the wrist. He's done nothing particularly wrong, has he? He's just piloted a boat. Not you— you've killed two men. No, you've killed three men. Why? Why kill them at all? You can tell me or not; either way, you're going to jail.' Macleod watched the woman bow her head, then she stood up, arching her back. She reminded him of a peacock, ready to strut.

'You're from here, aren't you? Seen your face; I've seen you in the press. You were the one who had the wife here, the one that died. You know what it's like, tiny hole. You don't get to be a big fish here, you just get to be a small fish that happens to be slightly bigger than the rest. I didn't want to be here. Carmichael was going to take me away; he said that when I was seventeen. Promised me, promised me until he'd been caught. Promised me until everyone knew what he was doing to me. Well, I didn't lose my dream. When I found out what Gemma was, when I understood why Alastair seemed to live in a house I could never afford, I saw my dream again.

'Alastair was as thick as anything, but Gemma, she had style. She knew what to do and what needed done and she got other people to do it. I needed a way in. I needed to be useful to her. I asked her what the big one was, what could get her the hell out of here. What could get her and Alastair away, and me, and she found it. She knows her art; she had her contacts. She worked them and she found it. She told me where it was and when it would be there and I whipped those boys into shape. They had the basic skills, skills of the trade but it took a year and a half to whip them into shape. To plan, to rehearse. Everything run through, out on that rig. Everything kept out on that rig. We did it, we damn well did it.'

'It went south,' said Macleod. 'What happened?'

'Angus Macleod was always lily-livered. He couldn't take the pressure, he told me. He told me he was going to buckle. I wouldn't mind it if he buckled once I'd got my money and got damn well out of there, but no, he's on that rig telling me. I set the fire and I told Alastair what to do. That's the thing about Alastair; he'd have done anything for Gemma and he'd do anything for me. He killed his best friend, his best friend from school. Hadn't seen each other until we got back together for the job, but he killed him. He cocked it up, of course. He was meant to throw him over the side, meant to put him in the sea, but no. He stuck him up with a bit of wire.

'Then you came along; you screwed it up too. That's the thing, you screwed it up. Caught him rummaging around, something else he couldn't do well. Should have done that myself, but then he was being chased and you were going to catch him. I had a dream, inspector; I had a dream. Nobody was going to stop it, but he'd screwed it up for me. I battered him. I hit him as hard as I could over and over again, and you know what? He didn't hit me back. Do you know what it's like, throwing your brother's body off an oil rig? I wanted it. I wanted the damn money.'

'You came back and still played it out, but you're not telling me something,' said Macleod. 'What about Carmichael?'

'Carmichael promised me the earth and he didn't deliver. Instead he ran— he ran when the rest of the world was going to know that he was screwing a school girl. I'll tell you straight, I wanted to do it from the minute I knew he still existed but we needed him. We needed another member and I blackmailed him into it. We needed somebody to take the money, somebody to move it down to the fence. I guess you know who that is by now, but once Carmichael had gone down, once he'd passed it on, that's when I told him no man walks out on me. You know what he said to me? I was just a bit of skank. Bastard. No man walks out on me, Inspector. Not him.'

Macleod motioned the officer beside him and she took Mairi Nicholson below into her cabin, to get her changed before taking her to the station. Across from Macleod, Michael was sitting by the steering controls and Macleod was watching the man shake.

'She would have killed me, too?' said Michael.

'Yes, she would,' said Macleod. Inside, he felt he'd saved at least one life.

Chapter 24

Macleod stood on the harbourside, looking down at the marina and the various yachts and small fishing craft that sat in the shimmering water. The sun was up again, and the temperature had climbed into doubled figures, causing Macleod to stand there in his shirt and tie, jacket held over his arm. There had been a day or two of roundup interviews, taking statements, and typing out reports, all done at the Stornoway station for ease before they would head back.

Today, the team had headed out for lunch, a celebratory one, something Macleod did now after every case. It was important to celebrate. Too often, the team had taken a battering, and you needed to remember the good times. As he had sat at lunch, he remembered they nearly lost Ross a few months ago, and so to see him sitting there in his good-natured fashion, genteel as always, smiling and laughing with the rest of the team, made Macleod feel warm inside. By standing, looking at the harbour he had seen so many times in his youth, he remembered his attitudes of yesteryear. He thought how times had changed. He wondered what the people from his village would have said if he told them in twenty years' time he'd been working with a gay man. *But that was the thing, wasn't it*, thought Macleod, *not to see him as a gay man. See Ross as a colleague, another officer. To see his female colleagues as officers, just other police officers, whatever their orientation, whatever their sex. Changed days, indeed.* Macleod was sure they were probably for the better.

He'd spent last night in an extremely long phone call to Jane, who, for some reason, was keen to redo the kitchen. Macleod was at that time of life when *keen to do DIY* did not happen and he inquired if she had priced up what it would cost to get a builder in. She had not. She probably saw it as a project. He would have to put his foot down on that one.

He continued to look out at the white yachts, including the now-detained yacht of Mairi Nicholson. Her Albanian pilot had been very helpful in explaining various parts of how the yacht had got there, who he had picked it out from, all in the trust that he could get back to Albania, unscathed by British justice. In truth, he was nobody in terms of the case. Macleod would push for him to be returned. In fact, Macleod was wondering just exactly what crime the man had committed. Could it be proven he knew the money was down there? Was he simply a sailor for hire or a besotted lover? It didn't matter. What mattered was Mairi Nicholson was going to get her just desserts. They had won again but not before time and three men were dead. What was it that had eaten inside the woman? What fire was there that when ignited would kill her brother? Macleod shook his head.

'What's up, boss?' It was Kirsten Stewart, and she seemed to be rather sheepish.

'Nothing,' said Macleod. 'I was just thinking about Mairi Nicholson. Such brutality on her brother. What urges go through you to do that? When does your lifestyle, money, become such a thing?'

'I think she's an exception.'

'A life as a copper says that's a lie.'

Stewart laughed, but then her face became serious. 'I did say I wanted to speak to you.'

'Well, you did,' said Macleod. 'Is this official? Do we need to go back to the station and sit down with a desk, and a pad and paper?'

'Well, it is going to be official.'

'I was sorry to hear about your brother. You were very close. It's not easy when you lose someone.'

'He's not dead, sir.'

'No, but your contact to him is, so he's effectively almost dead to you, can't recognize you. I was thinking it must have been similar to when I lost my wife. I believe she goes on, you see. It's a phase, isn't it? It's the trust you have. Life continues. There's something else beyond this. That's okay and that's a comfort, but you lose comms. You don't get to speak to them. I was thinking that's similar to you. Life goes on for your brother, but you don't get to speak to him, at least not as a sister anymore. I'm sorry. It must be hard to take.'

Macleod saw Kirsten take off her glasses and wipe her eyes. The woman rarely cried, but he saw the start of tears before she sniffed them back, put her glasses back on, before pushing them up on the bridge of her nose.

'It's a different day, sir. That's all. It's just a different day.'

'But you wanted to speak to me,' said Macleod. 'Sorry, I cut in. You want to talk to me about leaving.'

He saw the shock on Stewart's face. 'How did you know?'

'You're thorough as ever, but there's been something going

through your mind. I don't sit and watch my team all this time, Kirsten, without spotting things, and it makes sense. You've been approached by someone, haven't you?'

'Did they tell you? Did they come to you?'

'No, they didn't need to. If somebody from some other department had done it, I'd have been included somewhere along the line. They'd have asked me what you were like. Nobody has, but there's been a half gleam in you, an unsettling glimmer in your eye, something that you weren't sure of. Have you told them yes?'

'Not yet, sir. I wanted to talk to you first.'

'What? For my blessing? You don't owe me anything, Kirsten. You don't owe the team anything. We all pitch up. We do our part. When life moves on, life moves on; whether it's you, Hope, Ross, life moves on.'

'But I do owe you something. You lifted me out from being a constable to being the DC I am today, to being somebody that people wanted.'

'No, I didn't. I just saw something in you. I just put you in a place to shine. You did it. You need to understand that. It's you they've come for, not a version of me, not something that is controlled by me. It's you, your raw talent, your ability. They want someone who can fly solo, someone who can make decisions.'

Kirsten put her arms on the harbour railing and looked down at the boats. 'I don't feel like that person. You look like Mairi Nicholson's boat. It's massive, incredible, and I look like this little fisher, something people trundle through life in, I guess.'

'Day fisher. Trundle out in that; you can make a cup of tea in it, fish off the back, trundle back in.'

'I'm the day fisher,' said Stewart. 'Right there in the choppy water, not sure if it'll stay upright.'

'Nonsense,' said Macleod. 'You're well beyond that. You've gone through cases where you've been roughed up. Heck, Kirsten, we nearly lost you a couple of times if it hadn't been for your quick wits, your thinking. That's what they've seen—they've read the reports.'

'I haven't even told you who they are.'

'I know who they are. They're the ones that work in the dark. I've had contact over my years. They did ask me a while back now. I mean, look at me now. I'm too old for that. Back in the day, they did ask.'

'What did you say?'

Macleod looked across to Lews Castle across the harbour. There was a flag waving from the top of it, and he saw the trees that set up the camera image that all the tourists loved to shoot. 'I told them no. I think my exact words were, "God wanted everything out in the light."'

Kirsten looked at him. 'You said that?'

'Yes. You didn't know me in my younger days. I was a bit harsh then.'

'You can be a bit harsh now.'

'No. You're getting the light version.'

'Your faith kept you from doing it,' said Stewart.

'My faith kept me from nothing. My religiosity, my damn stupid religiosity kept me. My faith should have propelled me forward. People don't get that. People don't understand this thing I carry with me. Well, there's a few who do, but if you don't have faith, how do you understand it? I barely understand it myself.'

'Do you regret it, not taking it up?'

'Definitely,' said Macleod. 'Too late for me now. Now,

I'm just a grizzled, old police officer probably ready for the knacker's yard.'

'Don't say that, sir. This team needs you.'

'It does,' said Macleod, much to the Stewart's surprise. 'Hope's not ready. She's not far off, but she's not ready. She'll be fabulous at this one day in her own way, but your mind's wasted here. If you're asking me for permission, you don't need it. As they say in the maritime environment, it's at the master's discretion. You're the master of your ship. You decide where you go. Will we miss you? Every day, Kirsten, every day. With what's happened to your brother, it's the time to do it. Go and find what you really can be. Stop hiding in the shadows of the team. Go shine.'

Kirsten stepped forward and wrapped her arms around Macleod. 'Thank you.'

'For what?'

'For everything. I'll make you proud.'

'Hey,' said Macleod, 'anything you do, I'll never hear about.' He heard her laugh. 'Don't make me proud. Just go be damn good. Make the land a better place.'

Kirsten gave Macleod another hug and then walked off back towards the restaurant they'd come from. Macleod heard a little cough on the side. 'That all looked a little emotional. You don't give me hugs like that.' Macleod turned around and saw his red-headed colleague smiling with a hand on her hip. 'Not ready yet, am I, for the big seat?'

'No,' said Macleod, 'you're not ready.'

'Why is that?' asked Hope.

'Because the chair has to be vacant, and I'm not going anywhere yet.'

'Well, that's a turn up for the books. What's made that

decision?'

'What do you think of our kitchen, Hope? I mean, seriously.'

'To be honest, Seoras, I mean, I've been in that a few times, but it's nothing that's grabbed me.'

'Would you say it's functional?'

'As far as I know.'

'My thoughts exactly. Jane wants to change it and that's the problem, you see. If I give this up, I'm going to have to change every part of that house, but even then, she won't be happy. She'll find things for me to do. I need to stay here, otherwise I'll be DIY'ed out.'

Hope laughed, 'And Kirsten?'

'Moving on, best thing for her. She needs to be where you are and you're not going anywhere.'

'Who says?' said Hope.

'That John Allen fella. Yes, I can read you.' Hope laughed and even put a mild slap on the back of Macleod's shoulder. 'Back to the restaurant. We've still got to wind up today.' With that, Hope was off. Macleod looked out over the boats again. *To think she fell for the DIY thing. She really isn't ready*, thought Macleod. *I can't leave. This is what I do. This is me. Until I can't keep ahead of the game, this is me.*

Read on to discover the Patrick Smythe series!

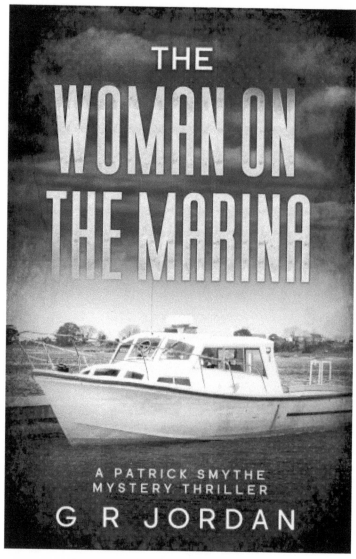

THE
WOMAN ON
THE MARINA

A PATRICK SMYTHE
MYSTERY THRILLER

G R JORDAN

Start your Patrick Smythe journey here!

Patrick Smythe is a former Northern Irish policeman who

after suffering an amputation after a bomb blast, takes to the sea between the west coast of Scotland and his homeland to ply his trade as a private investigator. Join Paddy as he tries to work to his own ethics while knowing how to bend the rules he once enforced. Working from his beloved motorboat 'Craigantlet', Paddy decides to rescue a drug mule in this short story from the pen of G R Jordan.

Join G R Jordan's monthly newsletter about forthcoming releases and special writings for his tribe of avid readers and then receive your free Patrick Smythe short story.

Go to https://bit.ly/PatrickSmythe for your Patrick Smythe journey to start!

About the Author

GR Jordan is a self-published author who finally decided at forty that in order to have an enjoyable lifestyle, his creative beast within would have to be unleashed. His books mirror that conflict in life where acts of decency contend with self-promotion, goodness stares in horror at evil, and kindness blindsides us when we at our worst. Corrupting our world with his parade of wondrous and horrific characters, he highlights everyday tensions with fresh eyes whilst taking his methodical, intelligent mainstays on a roller-coaster ride of dilemmas, all the while suffering the banter of their provocative sidekicks.

A graduate of Loughborough University where he masqueraded as a chemical engineer but ultimately played American football, Gary had worked at changing the shape of cereal flakes and pulled a pallet truck for a living. Watching vegetables freeze at -40'C was another career highlight and he was also one of the Scottish Highlands "blind" air traffic controllers.

These days he has graduated to answering a telephone to people in trouble before telephoning other people to sort it out.

Having flirted with most places in the UK, he is now based in the Isle of Lewis in Scotland where his free time is spent between raising a young family with his wife, writing, figuring out how to work a loom and caring for a small flock of chickens. Luckily, his writing is influenced by his varied work and life experience as the chickens have not been the poetical inspiration he had hoped for!

You can connect with me on:

🌐 https://grjordan.com

f https://facebook.com/carpetlessleprechaun

Subscribe to my newsletter:

✉ https://bit.ly/PatrickSmythe

Also by G R Jordan

G R Jordan writes across multiple genres including crime, dark and action adventure fantasy, feel good fantasy, mystery thriller and horror fantasy. Below is a selection of his work. Whilst all books are available across online stores, signed copies are available at his personal shop.

Fair Market Value (Highlands & Islands Detective Book 13)
An auctioneer beaten to death with a gavel. An elaborate scam to undervalue the work of a genius. Surrounded by a world he doesn't understand, can Macleod find the mysterious auction lot and bring a killer to justice?

Waving goodbye to the canny DC Stewart, Detective Inspector Macleod finds himself understaffed and lacking inspiration as he is immersed in the shadowy world of ancient artifacts. With talk of tradition and fantastical powers imbued by the stolen piece, the Inspector must separate whimsy and bluff from pure greed in order to find the perpetrator of a string of murders.

Going once - going twice - sold to the corpse in the corner!

Corpse Reviver (A Contessa Munroe Mystery #1)
https://grjordan.com/product/corspe-reviver

A widowed Contessa flees to the northern waters in search of adventure. An entrepreneur dies on an ice pack excursion. But when the victim starts moonlighting from his locked cabin, can the Contessa uncover the true mystery of his death?

Catriona Cullodena Munroe, widow of the late Count de Los Palermo, has fled the family home, avoiding the scramble for title and land. As she searches for the life she always wanted, the Contessa, in the company of the autistic and rejected Tiff, must solve the mystery of a man who just won't let his business go.

Corpse Reviver is the first murder mystery involving the formidable and sometimes downright rude lady of leisure and her straight talking niece. Bonded by blood, and thrown together by fate, join this pair of thrill seekers as they realise that flirting with danger brings a price to pay.

When no one else takes charge, the cream must rise to the top!

Highlands and Islands Detective Thriller Series
https://grjordan.com/
product/waters-edge
Join stalwart DI Macleod and his burgeoning new DC McGrath as they look into the darker side of the stunningly scenic and wilder parts of the north of Scotland. From the Black Isle to Lewis, from Mull to Harris and across to the small Isles, the Uists and Barra, this mismatched pairing follow murders, thieves and vengeful victims in an effort to restore tranquillity to the remoter parts of the land.

Be part of this tale of a surprise partnership amidst the foulest deeds and darkest souls who stalk this peaceful and most beautiful of lands, and you'll never see the Highlands the same way again

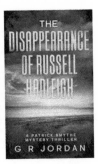

The Disappearance of Russell Hadleigh (Patrick Smythe Book 1)

https://grjordan.com/product/the-disappearance-of-russell-hadleigh

A retired judge fails to meet his golf partner. His wife calls for help while running a fantasy play ring. When Russians start co-opting into a fairly-traded clothing brand, can Paddy untangle the strands before the bodies start littering the golf course?

In his first full novel, Patrick Smythe, the single-armed former policeman, must infiltrate the golfing social scene to discover the fate of his client's husband. Assisted by a young starlet of the greens, Paddy tries to understand just who bears a grudge and who likes to play in the rough, culminating in a high stakes showdown where lives are hanging by the reaction of a moment. If you love pacey action, suspicious motives and devious characters, then Paddy Smythe operates amongst your kind of people.

Love is a matter of taste but money always demands more of its suitor.

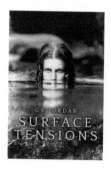

Surface Tensions (Island Adventures Book 1)

https://grjordan.com/product/surface-tensions

Mermaids sighted near a Scottish island. A town exploding in anger and distrust. And Donald's got to get the sexiest fish in town, back in the water.

"Surface Tensions" is the first story in a series of Island adventures from the pen of G R Jordan. If you love comic moments, cosy adventures and light fantasy action, then you'll love these tales with a twist. Get the book that amazon readers said, "perfectly captures life in the Scottish Hebrides" and that explores "human nature at its best and worst".

Something's stirring the water!